Crystal Mountain

BELLE DORMAN RUGH

Crystal Mountain

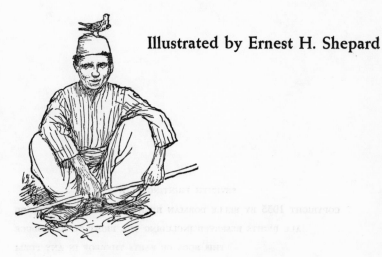

Illustrated by Ernest H. Shepard

HOUGHTON MIFFLIN COMPANY BOSTON

The Riverside Press Cambridge

Contents

Contents

To BETSY, MOLLY, and JUNE

Crystal Mountain

1 SURPRISE AT THE ROCKS

HARRY was lying across a rock on his stomach, looking at the Arabic primer open on the ground under his face. With a little twig from the oak tree overhead he touched the primer as he read and began spelling out Arabic syllables again: "Beh, dummy boo!"

A groan from above interrupted him. "Hush up! How do you expect me to *think* while you're making all that noise?"

"You're not supposed to be thinking," retorted Harry. "You're supposed to be studying French." He rolled over and sat up on the rock, suddenly looking up with interest at his brother perched on the biggest branch of the old tree. "So what are you thinking about?" he wanted to know.

"I was just thinking about Slanty Rocks, that's all," came the dignified answer. "And incidentally, I'm free to think. I've finished the chapter for today, and I think if this guy went around the world in eighty days, Jules Verne needn't have taken so many chapters to tell it. Phooey!"

And the French classic dropped with a bang on the clean-swept earth under the tree, followed by a pair of legs and a wiry body which dangled for a moment and then dropped.

"Come on," said Gerald. "You've learned that page and it's time for a hike."

"Do you think we could go alone this time to Slanty Rocks?" asked Harry as he picked up the primer, carefully placing an oak leaf in it to mark the page.

"Of course," was the reply. "Pa said we could if we got

back in time for dinner. So let's go through the house and leave the books as we go."

Down the stone steps they went from the flat terrace under the oak tree, and up a long flight of stairs to the house. Everything was stairs around this house built high in the Lebanon mountains above Beirut. Long stairs led up to it from the north and from the south; a wide flat terrace behind the house, where the boys played croquet, had stone steps leading up to it from both sides of the house. Beyond the side terrace, where the mountain rose steeply, little steps led up from one terrace of the vineyard to another, up to the tennis court at the very top of the vineyard. Here the climber could stop for a minute before starting the real scramble up the wild, rough mountainside. For from here on to the top of the cliff, the steps were only rough, uneven ones put there by nature and marked out in narrow paths made by the passing herds of goats.

The two boys had their own method of climbing the steps to the house. Instead of walking up like ordinary citizens they sped up on the *outside* of the iron railing to the top landing where one rail was conveniently missing, swerving through the hole and entering the house in a rush.

Through the hall they whirled, but slid to a sudden stop just at the entrance to the big central living room around which the house was built. They heard voices.

"Callers," groaned Gerald. "We heard 'em just in time. Come on, let's go around to the back door."

But it was too late. Their mother had heard them and was calling, "Boys! Come here, dears. I want you to meet Mrs. Wilkins."

With a look of despair, the two boys dragged wearily into the big court. This was a large room with high ceilings and a marble floor. On three sides the walls were lined with doors leading into other parts of the house. But the western end of the room was composed of high arched windows looking out over the village below. The two central windows reached to the floor and opened on to a balcony, overlooking the sea far below. At this end of the room, where a rug and easy chairs formed a comfortable island on the marble floor, their mother was sitting on the sofa next to a strange lady.

"Mrs. Wilkins," she said, "these are two of our boys, Gerald and Harry."

The visitor smiled at them languidly. "How sweet," she said. "What very big boys they are, aren't they? Quite frightening, really."

As this remark didn't seem to call for a reply, Gerald turned to his mother after an awkward pause, and said, "Ma, we are going up now to Slanty Rocks. O.K. if we get home by dinner time?"

Their mother smiled understandingly but as she started to nod her head, a sad voice interrupted.

"Oh dear me," drawled Mrs. Wilkins. "Little Dorothy will be so disappointed. The *paw* little thing has no one to play with, and I told her that she might come up here to play when her lessons were done. You see," she added, turning to the boys' mother, "I heard that you had little children up here, and I thought it would be *so* nice — " Her voice trailed off for a moment. The "little children" gazed at each other in dismay. Mrs. Wilkins' weary voice went on. "Little Dorothy's mother is ill; they live in Egypt too, you know, so I asked Dorothy to spend the summer with us. Her governess is with her, so she's no trouble, but things are rather dull here for little girls."

Then Mrs. Wilkins glanced at her watch and added gaily, "But she should be here now. It's ten already, and she stops her lessons at hop-pus nine. I told her to meet me here at ten."

"Children," suggested their mother, "why don't you go outside and see if she is coming?" Her eyes followed them sympathetically as they trailed out of the house.

Mrs. Wilkins' voice faded behind them, continuing to drawl. "*Rilly* I don't know why little Dorothy is so late: I get so *tahd* trying to decide what she's to do — "

"Well, there goes our trip to Slanty Rocks!" snorted Harry. "We'll have to spend the morning playing parcheesi with little Dorothy."

"How *sweet!*" mimicked Gerald.

"Quite frightening, really," added Harry. "She must have been looking at your hair, Gel. It's looking like a whisk-broom again in front."

By now the boys were standing at the top of the stairs again, looking down the road. Momentarily cheered by their mimicry, they relapsed into a morose mood.

The sun beat down warmly on their backs as they settled on the top step to wait, and the spicy fragrance of thyme and other wild bushes drifted enticingly down from the mountainside. From the kitchen came the thump, thump of the wooden pestle as the cook pounded some meat for dinner. Still the road stretched white and empty below, till it disappeared around the curve of the hillside. And the glorious morning full of adventure and possibilities ahead of them now had collapsed into a dull and empty waste of time to be gotten through. Harry slumped despondently against the railing, moodily watching a small lizard poke its head up into the sun over the step.

"Little Dorothy *ought* TO LEARN to be on time!" Something in Gerald's voice made Harry glance hopefully up at him. Gerald's eyes were twinkling.

"Look! Mrs. Wilkins told her to be here at ten, and she isn't here. So how can we help it if we can't wait any longer? We've waited and waited — why it must be three minutes after ten, and she isn't even in sight."

"Let's go!" said Harry happily, jumping up. "Ma knows where we are going so we don't have to speak to her again, and maybe we'd better not disturb them in there."

Once the decision was made, the boys lost no time. Carefully avoiding any backward glances at the road below, they took the path up to the tennis court. In a short time they were high on the mountain behind the house. Here they stopped for breath, resting a moment on one of the blue-gray boulders near the mountain path. Up here there were no trees to shelter them from the sun, and any tufts of grass that had grown up between the rocky boulders had long since been dried to a straw-yellow by the long summer sun. Yet the breeze that blew up the mountain from the sea was cooling, and sweet with the fragrance of sage and thyme which had tempted them a few minutes earlier. The only green spots on the mountain side were the bushes of broom, which here and there still had a spike of yellow blossoms shining on them; and low on the ground were the gray-green bushes which gave off the fragrant mountain perfume. At first there seemed to be no sound at all up there except the boys' own deep sighs as they caught their breath. Presently the sounds of the village far below became noticeable: a man pounding a nail, a mother calling her baby, the faint clop-clop of a donkey's feet, the jingling of its bells all came clearly to the boys' ears.

Gerald turned and looked up at the top of the mountain where a line of huge boulders formed a sort of wall. Some rocks were tipped sideways and looked as if they might fall at any moment, but the bushes and small stunted pine trees growing around and on top of them showed that they had been poised there for many years. Above the cliffs, where the mountainside sloped gently back to the summit, the slope was covered with small pines — some as high as a man, most of them smaller; growing precariously out of the rocky soil. "Come on!" said Gerald. "We're near the top."

There was not much talking as the boys scrambled up the last steep stretch. When the path brought them to the foot of the cliffs it turned and followed the foot of the rocks around the shoulder of the mountain. When the boys came to the shoulder, they stopped again. Here an angle of the cliff above them formed a bit of shade which was fast receding as the sun moved directly overhead.

"We're almost there now!" said Harry as they hurried on around the mountain. "I'd like to see Mrs. Wilkins catch us now. There they are!"

Before the boys rose the massive pile of rocks which they had named Slanty Rocks. The pines abruptly stopped here, and the goat path seemed to dwindle away into nothing. Great rocks of blue-gray limestone, many of them as big as a house, were tumbled together helter-skelter as if some ancient giant's castle had suddenly crashed into a heap. Some stood straight up and high like columns or towers against the sky; some were as flat as a huge table top; some stood at crazy angles like exhausted runners leaning against each other. To the boys it was like some ancient ruined city. They were very quiet now, as they approached the rocks. The village below was hidden from view as they had rounded the mountainside, so the village sounds had faded and the place seemed very still. Their sneakers were almost soundless going along the path. Here they heard only the bees buzzing around the bushes. Once a little stone rattled down from above and the boys jumped — then looked at each other sheepishly when they saw a lizard disappearing into a bush.

"First let's get up on that flat-topped rock," suggested Gerald, "and have our eats."

Some quick climbing brought them up there, and digging into his pocket, Gerald brought out the rations and spread them on the clean rock. There was a large piece of flat Arab bread; this he opened to reveal four black olives and a slice of white goat's cheese. The bread was divided carefully; and each boy took two olives and half of the cheese.

"It's a lonely sort of place, isn't it?" said Harry. "Do you suppose anybody ever comes here?"

"Not now any more," said Gerald. "Even the goats like other slopes better. More green stuff to eat."

"What do you mean 'any more'?" demanded Harry.

"Well — " said Gerald — "Remember the sarcophagus Pa showed us? A thousand years ago people used rocks like these to carve out coffins, sort of, and bury their dead in them. There are probably quite a lot of ancient broken ones here among these rocks."

"But did people *live* here too do you suppose?" asked Harry. "They're good big useful rocks, and some of them *look* like houses."

"Good places to hide in," said Gerald. "Robbers could have lived here," he added carelessly.

"You mean recently?"

"Oh not *now*," said Gerald scornfully. "Maybe a hundred years ago. Nobody lives here now. Only jackals. We can hear them at night from our back porch, howling up here on the mountain on moonlight nights. They sound like children wailing. They live among rocks like these."

"Isn't it time for us to be starting home about now?" said Harry, suddenly conscientious.

"But we just *got* here," said Gerald. "Let's explore." He stood up and Harry, more reluctantly, rose also — then suddenly both boys stood still as if they had been paralyzed. An unearthly wail split the air; then the voice grew softer and sadder until the wail died away.

"Could — could that have been a jackal?" asked Harry in a whisper.

"I don't *think* so. No it *couldn't*," replied Gerald decidedly. "They are afraid of the daylight."

The boys stood uncertainly on the rock with the sun blazing down on them. Far away they could see the glimmer of the sea, and the bees were buzzing quietly around them, as if nothing had happened.

"Do bees have ears?" asked Harry in an undertone.

"You *do* ask the silliest questions sometimes," said Gerald sharply. "Now come along if you want to. I'm going to see what that noise is. Stay here and wait for me if you like. What are we whispering for, anyway?"

From the flat rock where they had been sitting Gerald crawled up a long inclined ledge which looked like a huge ironing board pointed up into the air. Harry hesitated a moment, then followed him reluctantly.

When he reached the top of the ironing board, Gerald flattened out and peered over the edge. He lay there so long without moving that Harry became curious. He crept up after him and peered over. Below them was a clear space between the high tumbled rocks, forming a sort of room with the sky for a roof. At the far side of this space was a dark hole. But what held the boys' attention were two brown legs protruding out of the hole. The owner was lying on his stomach with his head in the hole.

"Do you suppose he's dead, or stuck down there?" asked Harry.

But the legs waved in the air as he spoke, answering the first half of the question, and the owner of the legs, heaving up on his knees slightly, wiggled himself farther in. Then suddenly came the wail again; more muffled now, but unmistakably from the hole.

"Hey!" said Gerald sternly to the legs.

The legs waved wildly, the body emerged, and a very angry face whirled around at them. Red pigtails whirled around, too, and one furious word came out.

"*Boys!*"

"What are you making all that racket for?" yelled Gerald, still shaking a little both with anger and with relief.

"None of your silly business!" screamed the redhead. "You've spoiled it now anyway!"

Muttering to herself, the girl scrambled to her feet and brushed the earth off her skirts as the boys watched in silence. Now that she was standing up, they could see that she was somewhat shorter than Harry, though her long brown legs under the short blue dress she wore gave her a spindly air. Presently she glanced up at them and surprised them both by bursting out into a gale of laughter.

"If you could see yourselves up there! Just two heads against the blue sky; all you need is a pair of wings apiece and you could be cherubs smiling down upon me — if you smiled, that is."

Both the boys scrambled up on their knees at this, and began backing down off the rock. Gerald shouted angrily to the girl, who was momentarily out of sight, "Well if we're angelic looking, let me tell you you certainly sounded like something quite different, down there in that hole."

Suddenly he stopped his backward scrambling and turned to face Harry with his eyes narrowed. "Come closer," he whispered. Harry edged up the rock till his face was close to Gerald's.

"That girl talks as if she were English. And personally I don't know any English families around here unless —" He paused impressively. "Do you suppose that THAT" (he moved his head in the general direction of the howler) "could be little Dorothy?"

Harry's jaw dropped. Then he said determinedly, "There's only one way to find out. And you're the oldest. Go ask her."

At the cost of a few scrapes on their knees, the boys were soon down off the rock. Leading the way around it Gerald came face to face with the redhead. "Now just who are you? What's your name?" he demanded severely, trying to forget he had just been compared to a cherub.

The girl hesitated. "I was here first, so you might tell me your name first."

"All right," proceeded Gerald grimly. "My name is Gerald and this is my brother Harry. Now — what's your name?"

"Boadicea," was the reply. "You can call me Boadie for short, though, if you want to."

"Boadie. What sort of a name is that?" inquired Gerald.

"Boadicea was an early British queen," explained the girl with dignity. "And she was a fighter too. Led an army against the Roman invaders. It's a good name — not a silly girl's name like Betty or Jane or Dorothy." Gerald and Harry started and looked foolishly at each other as she mentioned the last name. But Boadie was paying no attention. "Now look," she went on. "Since we're here we might as well have some fun together. Come along."

"First," said Gerald, who wasn't to be diverted easily, "suppose you tell us just why you were howling into that hole."

"Oh, that," said Boadie uneasily. "Just an idea. I wanted to see a jackal. I've heard 'em up here on the mountain at night but I've never seen one. Thought if I sang sweetly to them one of them might come crawling up to see what it was."

"Sweetly!" exclaimed Harry.

Boadie grinned. "I've been practicing. You'll admit I sound like a jackal. *They* think it's sweet. — Yew-ew-ew-ew!"

The mournful wail came so suddenly the boys jumped — but in a moment they both joined in. Then they all stopped out of breath.

"See how quiet it is all of a sudden?" said Boadie. "The jackals are jealous of our music."

It certainly was quiet there. The children held their breaths and listened. The great rocks shut them into the little circle where they stood.

"Do you know," said Boadie softly, "I'm glad you're here. It could get a bit lonely around these rocks after a while."

She bent over and picked a bit of sage. Crushing it between her fingers she sniffed it and asked the boys, "Can you keep a secret?"

"Of course," they replied together. Gerald added conscientiously, "Unless it's something illegal or underhanded."

Boadie looked at him. "Of course it isn't. Come on, then, I'll show you *my* rock."

"It's a good thing you're not fat," she added as she led the way around a large rock opposite the ironing board and into a narrow crevice between two very high walls. Here the narrow passage had been half filled with a pile of smaller rocks at the far end. These formed a sort of rough stairway up which Boadie proceeded, followed by the two boys. Above the top of the pile, on the wall to the right, a narrow ledge appeared. Boadie climbed on to this and led the way around to the other side of a high, towerlike projection. Here the ledge opened out to a wide, flat balcony. Below the rock, the ground fell steeply away, with smaller rocks lying in profusion down the slope. And far below, spread valleys and in the distance shone the sea. Boadie sat down.

"Here is the balcony. Relax," she invited them. The boys looked at each other and smiled as they sat down.

"Gee, thanks," said Gerald. "So this is *your* rock!"

"Certainly," said Boadie. "I just discovered it this morning. But I'm glad to invite you onto it," she added generously. "As long as you observe the rules."

"What rules?" inquired Harry.

"Ah," said Boadie. "Look here." She crawled to the rim of the balcony where a crack led down over the edge. "Feel in there," she ordered.

Harry put his hand in, somewhat gingerly. "There's a piece of paper in there!" he exclaimed.

"Pull it out," said Boadie excitedly, sitting back on her

heels. "Read it," she demanded.

Harry pulled it out. It was a piece of note-paper, folded over three times, and on it was written the following which Harry read out loud:

> "*Rules For Sitting on this Rock*
>
> *Do not throw papers around.*
> *No smoking. Fire regulations.*
> *Dogs cordially invited.*
> *Do not molest the ants on this rock.*
> *No boys allowed here.*"

As Harry read the last regulation, Boadie gave a little exclamation of dismay.

"Oh I'm sorry, I forgot about that last rule." She pulled a stub of pencil out of her pocket, and taking the paper, hastily added a word to the last line. Then she held it up for the boys to see, saying with a smile, "*Now* it's all right isn't it?"

They looked at the corrected regulation that now read: "No American boys allowed here."

"But we are Americans," said Harry.

"You're never!" Boadie gazed at them in consternation. "You couldn't be! — I mean — oh dear. You see I never met any American kids. I've taken good care not to. They wanted me to meet some loathsome American children when we came to the mountains but I escaped. Look — I'll just cross out that last rule altogether." This she did, and then folding up the paper again she replaced it in the crack.

While she was doing this, Gerald and Harry were making mysterious gestures at each other — Gerald raising his eyebrows, and Harry smiling back, and finally both of them nodding in agreement.

"Boadie," said Gerald, "We think that since you have

shared your secret with us we'll let you in on one of ours."

Boadie flushed with pleasure, and rubbed her freckled nose with one finger, so as not to show how pleased she was.

"You mean another rock?" she asked politely.

"No. This one," said Gerald. "You see your rock has been inhabited before."

"Let me show her," said Harry.

"Of course it's been a year," said Gerald. "Maybe it has gone." The two boys were on their knees now, examining the surface near the ledge that led to the balcony.

"Here it is!" exclaimed Harry. A deep arrow scratched into the surface of the rock, pointed straight over the ledge. Lying on his stomach, Harry put his whole arm over the edge and felt around. His comments kept the others informed.

"The little bush is still there — I feel it! And here's the hole above it. And — yes, it's still there! Here it is!" Triumphantly he brought his arm up and clutched in his hand was a small tin pillbox. Ceremoniously he handed it to Boadie who sat down and inspected it, the two boys squatting on either side of her eagerly. She examined it. "It says 'Bayer's Aspirin,'" she said. Then she shook it.

"Oh go ahead. *Open* it," said Gerald impatiently.

The tin seemed a little rusty, but with some help from Gerald's pocketknife, it gave way. Inside were one Lincoln penny and a few wisps of hair. Boadie looked a little disappointed.

"That's an interesting coin," she said politely.

"A penny," said Harry. "New last year."

"No it's not a penny," contradicted Boadie. "It's a cent. Look, it says so."

Harry laughed. "We call them pennies," he explained.

"May I ask what the hair is?" asked Boadie.

"It's a sort of relic," said Gerald. "One wisp of hair is Harry's and one is mine. You see years from now, when we are famous men, people can come and find samples of our hair."

He looked at Boadie to see if she would laugh. But she did not. "I think that's a very interesting idea," she said. Gerald relaxed. Boadie seemed to be a girl of sense.

"If you would care to pull out a few wisps of your hair, we'd be glad to add yours to the tin."

Boadie smiled with pleasure. "I'd simply love it, and thank you very much," she said. Quickly she pulled several hairs out of the end of one pigtail, twisted them around one finger into a little curl, and added the bit of shining red to the blond wisps already in the box. Gerald closed the box, and stretching out on his stomach, carefully replaced it in the hidden hole.

"Of course you understand it's quite a secret," he added. "You know if anybody heard about it — I mean grown-ups — "

"I know," said Boadie, and the boys felt reassured.

"And now we've got to go," said Gerald. "We're going to be awfully late for dinner. Where do you live, Boadie?"

"Over there," she said, waving vaguely in the direction of the sea. "I expect I'd better not walk down to the village with you on the regular path. I'm not supposed to come up here alone, you see. Or with strange boys," she added with a grin.

"Can't you come up again tomorrow?" asked Harry. "We could meet you here."

"Not unless I bring Dunbar along," said Boadie gloomily. "I'll never get away like this again."

"Who's Dunbar?" asked Harry.

Boadie laughed. "Really I don't think I'd better tell you who Dunbar is until you have a chance to meet each other. Dunbar's not bad. And I know I can be here if Dunbar's along. You'll have a real surprise. Look!" she said, changing the subject. "I'll meet you tomorrow under that tall pine tree at the edge of the Rocks."

The boy's eyes followed her pointing finger. There was only one really tall old pine tree which stood up against the sky, on the ridge of cliffs.

"All right," said Gerald. "Which way do you go?"

"I go above the cliffs and then down farther along," said Boadie. "So ta-ta for now." She started to scramble down the rock ledge. The boys followed her. Gerald called after her — "How in the world did your parents ever think of calling you that odd name?"

Boadie was now scrambling down the "staircase" but she called back over her shoulder, "They didn't. I named myself."

"You what?" called Gerald.

"I named myself. Did you ever hear of the Amatan tribe of Siberia? In that tribe the children choose their own names when they are ten years old."

Now Boadie was crossing the space near the jackal hole, and the boys were hurrying after her. "So your real name isn't Boadie-whatever-it-is?" said Gerald.

"Of course it's my real name!" came the reply. "My mother is an Amatan, and I named myself. I've got to hurry now, though, or they'll be calling me something else when they find I've been gone so long!"

In a few moments the boys were tramping along the path around the mountain. The figure in the blue dress had disappeared over the hill.

After supper that night Gerald looked up from the encyclopedia when a name struck his ear. His father and mother had been talking together.

"*Who* did you say was here to tea, mother?" he asked.

"Miss Dunbar, dear. The governess for little Dorothy Wilcox. She didn't stay long, though. She was worried about something."

Gerald bent a bewildered face over the encyclopedia. Presently he spoke to his mother again.

"Is this encyclopedia up to date?"

"I don't know, dear. Why?"

"I can't seem to find anything about the Amatan tribes."

"Never heard of them," said his father.

Gerald slammed the encyclopedia shut, with a shout of laughter.

"Now what is the matter dear?" asked his mother.

"Amatans!" He exclaimed. "I'm just wondering whether little Dorothy has red hair!"

Girls are girls after all," said Gerald gloomily. "She seemed O.K., but you can't trust them."

It was just after breakfast and the two boys were sitting on the edge of the outdoor cistern, dangling their legs over the green water. A frog sticking his head out below them disappeared with a splash, but the boys paid no attention. Their thoughts were on the trickery of a redheaded girl.

"She knew we wouldn't come if she told us Miss Dunbar was a governess."

"*Amatans* indeed! Phooey!" Gerald's voice was heavy with scorn, but his eyes turned up to the mountain and focused on the outline of a tall pine on the high cliff.

"See anybody moving up there?" asked Harry anxiously.

"No. Who cares anyway?" Gerald with a great show of nonchalance pulled his legs up out of the cistern and stood up. "Come on!" he said. "Let's go see what Pa's doing over there."

The boys jumped off the wall and ambled along the terrace under the scattered shade of the fig trees, to a small quince tree at the end. At the base of the tree their father was sitting on his heels, absorbed as he inspected a hole in the bark. Fine fresh sawdust spilled out of the hole, forming a little pile on the ground.

"See that fresh sawdust?" said their father. "He's right in there now working away. Going to kill this little tree if we don't stop him."

The boys squatted on either side of their father. He stood up, pulled out a sharp penknife, opened it and squatted down again. Gently he began to prod in the hole, talking to himself as he worked.

"Nope, this hole goes way in. We'll have to cut away some of the wood."

Carefully, with a surgeon's delicacy and sureness, he began to lay open the hole, cutting enough of the wood away to open up the tunnel. He worked patiently and intently. The shade from the little quince tree was not enough to protect the three from the sun that beat down on their necks.

"Pa," said Gerald, finally.

"Hrrup," was the amiable if somewhat abstract reply, while the operation continued. The doctor had pulled a wire out of his pocket, and was pushing it up the hole.

"Pa, we told Dorothy Wilcox yesterday that we'd go and meet her on the mountain this morning."

"Well, what are you doing here then?" Jab, jab went the wire, up into the tree.

"We don't want to go. She told us her name was something else and she's bringing her *governess* along. So we're not going — Do we have to?" he ended somewhat abruptly.

Their father stood up and wiped his chin, and looked at Gerald. He had on his outdoor glasses with a steel frame and though his tone was serious Gerald wasn't sure whether the blue eyes had a twinkle in them, as he replied, "Well, a gentleman always keeps his word to a lady."

"But *she's* not a lady!" argued Harry eagerly. "She pretends things that aren't so. Is that ladylike?"

"Well now, I can't speak for the ladies," calmly replied their father, taking off his spectacles and polishing them.

"You'll have to ask your mother."

He squatted down again, the boys beside him, and continued his work. Presently, "Here he is!" he exclaimed as a fat white borer worm dropped into his hand. The boys examined him with distaste, and the three headed toward the house to display their trophy to their mother.

Ten minutes later the boys were heading up the mountain path.

"Anyway I don't feel like a gentleman," said Harry.

"I think the ladies get away with murder," grumbled Gerald. Nevertheless, in spite of their grumbling, they hurried along with apparent eagerness, glancing ahead now and then to the towering cliffs above them.

As they neared the cliffs, the climb became steeper and their steps slower. Here the path turned and ran along the foot of the cliff, and soon they were standing under the point where the pine tree towered above them. A short scramble up the crevice between the rocks brought them up to the base of the tree. Here the boys looked at each other with an odd mixture of relief and chagrin. The place was utterly deserted. The wind sighed through the pine needles above them. A crow swooped down from the blue sky, and flew far below them over the village, the "caw! caw!" of its cries growing fainter, as it coasted down on the invisible air currents, and far away. Suddenly both the boys turned. Two or three pebbles had rolled down the slope above them, and following the direction they saw, a few feet away, two brown legs sticking out from behind a clump of heather.

"What a dumb idea! Hiding on us!" exclaimed Harry.

The only reply was a "Sh!" from behind the bush, and following the legs, they came upon Boadie, again flat on her stomach, apparently absorbed in examining the earth.

"Do you spend all your time on your stomach when we're not around?" demanded Gerald.

"Oh be quiet!" was the reply. "Get down here and watch what's going on."

Both boys squatted down and followed her pointing finger. A small black ant was struggling to carry a large dead wasp. For a few seconds it tugged and pulled with no results; then after a few encouraging words from the children, suddenly it picked it up wildly and ran a little way with it until it reached a little stone. Then down went the burden and again the tugging began. First the ant tried lifting its prize up over the little stone.

"Not there, stupid!" exclaimed Boadie. "Go around!"

"Let's move the stone," suggested Harry.

"No," said Gerald. "That would only confuse him and make him run off in a different direction. Anyway *he* knows where he wants to go and we don't."

"Stop saying 'he,'" lectured Boadie. "The ants that do the work are all girls. The male ants are practically useless. They just sit around and get fat. Typical!" she added.

This remark was greeted with silence. They watched while the ant tugged this way and that. Then suddenly it seemed to make up its mind, and getting a good grip on its trophy it dragged it around the little stone. The three children stood up and suddenly Gerald remembered something.

"How come Miss Dunbar isn't here with you?" he inquired rather severely.

"Miss Dunbar? Oh, you know about her?" asked Boadie, a little disappointed.

"Certainly we do. And we don't think much of playing

around with a governess to look after us like babies!"

"Be quiet! You'll hurt her feelings if she hears you!" said Boadie.

The boys looked around again but the mountainside seemed as deserted as ever.

"*Now* what's the joke?" demanded Gerald. "I don't believe she's here at all."

But Boadie had moved over to the base of the pine tree and beckoning to the boys, pointed up into the tree. The boys moved over and looked up. The pine tree whispered softly in the breeze, and at first the boys noticed nothing. The wide lower branches reached peacefully out over the cliff. But as their eyes traveled up the trunk to the top they saw, where the pine needles stood out against the blue sky, a neatly dressed lady sitting on a branch with her back against the trunk. Her feet rested on a smaller branch below her, and on her nose rested a pair of pince-nez glasses. She appeared to be reading. Her long, trim brown skirt reached to her ankles. The boys stared in astonishment. Gerald was the first to speak. In an awed whisper he inquired, "What's she doing? How did she get up there? Is she crazy or something?"

Boadie chuckled. "Better not let her hear you say that! She certainly is not crazy. She just has more sense than most grownups."

"But why is she up *there?*" asked Gerald.

"Don't *you* ever climb trees?" demanded Boadie impatiently.

This sensible question seemed to require no answer. As the boys continued to stare up into the tree, the lady closed the book, slipped it into a large pocket in her skirt, removed her pince-nez and called down, "Dorothy!"

"Yes, Miss Dunbar?"

"You have friends down there?"

"Yes, Miss Dunbar. These are the boys I told you about."

"I should like to meet them. I'll be right down."

In a leisurely fashion she began descending the tree as

serenely as if she were walking downstairs. Now the boys could see that the long skirt was divided into wide trousers. As Miss Dunbar swung down from the last branch and stood before them, the trousers fell into place, again looking like an ordinary wide, long skirt.

"Gerald, I am glad to meet you. And how do you do, Harry?" She shook hands with each of them. Gerald replied politely, but Harry forgot to reply at all. He was trying to decide whether this was an old lady or a young one. Her skirt was too long for a very young lady, but then it wasn't really a skirt. Her hair was gray under a straight-brimmed brown hat pinned firmly to her hair with a hatpin but she had long black eyelashes and very clear gray eyes.

Gerald nudged him. "Can't you answer?"

"Oh — how do you do?" replied Harry belatedly.

Miss Dunbar was exploring the depths of the big pocket in her skirt. She looked up at Harry and smiled.

"Would you boys care to join us in our elevenses?" she asked.

"Well, thanks," said Gerald cautiously, not knowing what the invitation meant.

"Here's a good table!" announced Boadie, patting a low flat rock nearby.

From her pocket Miss Dunbar produced a small box of crackers and a little package of raisins. These she set on the "table" and the four sat around it for a snack.

"What did you call this?" inquired Gerald.

"Elevenses," said Miss Dunbar. "It's a useful English custom. At eleven you have a snack so you can carry on till lunch time."

"Gerald and I have that custom too," said Harry. "But we didn't know it had a name."

Boadie was brushing up the crumbs from the rock and carrying them over to the spot where their ant had struggled with the dead wasp.

"Maybe he'll come back and find the crumbs here," she explained.

"She, you mean," corrected Gerald happily.

Boadie smiled.

"And now," said Miss Dunbar, standing up briskly, "It is time for an hour's free activity." The boys stared at her. She talked as if they were in a schoolroom. "Dorothy," she continued, "have you written up your observations?"

"No," said Dorothy dolefully. "I was still observing when the boys came. First I observed the anthill, and then I found this ant with a wasp — "

"Well, wait!" said Miss Dunbar. "As the observation took longer today, you may write it up tomorrow. Just jot down some of the main facts in the notebook, so you won't forget them. Then we'll be off."

Boadie pulled a small notebook out of her pocket. A stubby pencil was attached to it with a piece of string. Sitting down on the rock table, she opened the notebook.

"What things might I forget?" she inquired.

"How large an ant was it?" asked Miss Dunbar briskly. "Just draw a line to show its size."

Dorothy drew a line. Then she added feelers and six legs.

"Was it red or black?"

"Black," said Boadie, writing it down.

"How long did you watch it, and how far did it travel?"

Boadie wrote: "20 minutes. Traveled about five times the length of this notebook."

"Any other special points to remember?"

Boadie wrote: "Describe wasp. Actions when stone was

in the way. Ali the milk man."

Gerald, who was looking over her shoulder, demanded, "What has Ali got to do with it?"

"Just a reminder for myself," replied Boadie briefly. "How the ant looked when he dropped the wasp and waved his hands around excitedly in the air."

"She," said Gerald automatically. "*Her* hands."

"He," said Boadie. "Ali's hands. When he's excited."

During the last few remarks Miss Dunbar had walked back to the tree to pick up a portfolio which was resting against the trunk. The argument was closed by her announcing firmly, "I am off to finish the sketch I started yesterday above the old house. Dorothy, your lessons are finished for today and you may play anywhere as long as you remain within sight."

Gerald's eyes wandered off to the valleys and mountains stretching out below them to the seaside plain far beyond. He thought to himself, Well, that leaves Boadie plenty of space to play in! But aloud he only asked, "What old house?"

Miss Dunbar pointed down the slope to the right of the mountains, where there was a clump of small pine trees.

"A bit below the cliff there, see?"

Gerald didn't need to look where her finger pointed.

"I know," he said; "that's the Mystery House."

"*Is* it?" asked Boadie excitedly. "Has it really got a mystery? Is the house haunted?"

Gerald looked a little sheepish. "We just call it that," he replied. "But isn't it a mystery, anyway, why anyone would build so far up on the mountain, away from the rest of the village, and far from the village fountain?"

Boadie looked a little disappointed. But she answered

hopefully, "Well anyway, let's follow Dunbar and explore the house carefully while she is sketching. Maybe there *is* a mystery there of some kind. If not, we can start one ourselves."

She had jumped up and now started along the stony mountain path. Miss Dunbar was already some distance ahead, and the two boys followed in a leisurely fashion, kicking the loose stones in the path as they went. Gerald murmured confidentially to Harry as they went along, "There's nothing to *explore* there — a little one-room house like that, with the roof fallen in, and we've been there millions of times. But we might as well let her see for herself."

A few minutes later they had reached the clump of pine trees. Just below them was the little ruined house.

"I shall sit right here," declared Miss Dunbar, settling herself on a little ledge under the pines. Taking her glasses case from her pocket she laid it on the ground beside her as she opened her portfolio. Boadie was already running down the slope to the little house, but the boys lingered to see what Miss Dunbar was going to do. She had taken out a box of crayons and pencils, and set them down on the other side of her, and now she was taking out the sketch.

"Would you like to see it? There!" she said in a pleased tone holding it up for the boys.

The boys stared at it silently. There seemed to be a great many lines and circles of color in the picture, but it didn't look much like the view from the mountain.

"Well," said Gerald politely, "thanks for letting us see it."

"You don't like it much, do you?" said Miss Dunbar directly. "Don't be embarrassed. I'm not trying to sketch this view exactly as it looks, you see. I'm trying to show how *I* feel about it. It's an experiment."

"Well, I guess I don't feel about the mountain that way," said Gerald, looking doubtfully at the mixture of colors.

"Naturally not," retorted Miss Dunbar. "Nobody feels the same way about this mountain. A farmer looks at it and says, 'What a terrible place to raise a crop!' He sees the rocks and the thin soil and the steep slopes. That ant you saw feels differently. 'A lovely place!' he thinks. 'Lots of little dried seeds and dead wasps and very few people to trample on me.' But that's not what the jackal feels about it. He says to himself — Now where did I put my eyeglasses?"

Somewhat startled, Gerald replied: "You put them down on the ledge beside you, on the other side."

"I thought I did," said Miss Dunbar. "But they're gone."

She stood up and shook out her long trousers. Gerald and Harry peered around on the ledge and below it, but there was no sign of the glasses case.

"Did you put them in your pocket while we were talking?" asked Gerald.

Miss Dunbar fished up everything that was in her large pocket and set it out on the ledge. It was quite a display: the small box of raisins, now nearly empty, the cracker box, a large Boy Scout knife, a tin box clearly labeled "First Aid," a neatly tied piece of string, a clean handkerchief, a pocket compass, and a book that had "Homer's *Odyssey*" printed in large letters on the cover. But no eyeglasses.

Miss Dunbar said rather severely, "You boys didn't take them?"

Gerald and Harry were indignant.

"That would be a stupid sort of joke!" said Gerald. He looked sternly in the direction of the little house, where Boadie had disappeared.

But Harry rushed to her defense. "Boadie didn't even come up on the ledge," he pointed out. "She took the short cut below."

Miss Dunbar shook her head. "The thing *can't* have disappeared when it was here in plain sight, and yet it has! What a mystery!"

"The first mystery of the Mystery House," said Harry cheerfully.

Miss Dunbar did not look amused. Gerald was making another minute search of the ledge. It seemed only polite to try again, though it did seem useless. Suddenly he exclaimed. "Look! I think I've found where it is!"

On top of the ledge there was an uneven place where one layer of rock formed a slightly higher level than the level on which they were sitting. The edge of this higher level stuck out a little over the lower level. Gerald's hand was in there. When he brought it out, his hand was still empty.

"Feel in there!" he said.

Miss Dunbar and Harry both stuck their hands in, expecting to bump into the glasses case. Instead their fingers reached into a wide crack which went right down into the rock.

Miss Dunbar sat up. "Well that's that. How can we ever get them out of there?"

"Wait!" said Gerald. "Let's see how deep this crack is!" He had picked up a small stone and was poking it under the edge. He lay down on his stomach and put his ear to the crack.

"Come and listen!" he said.

Miss Dunbar and Harry also lay down and put their ears to the crack. Gerald pushed the stone in. They could hear it rattling down for a second, then silence, then a faint smack as it hit bottom somewhere far below them.

"My word!" muttered Miss Dunbar. "There must be a big hole down there."

A sudden voice above them made them all turn around and sit up.

"What in the world!" exclaimed Boadie indignantly. "I've been calling and calling to you — And you say *I* spend all my time lying on my stomach! What's going on anyway?"

Briefly Gerald explained the situation. Of course Boadie had to lie down promptly and drop a stone down the crack. Meanwhile, Miss Dunbar was regretfully repacking her pocket and putting her sketching things back into the portfolio.

"It's no use trying to do anything without my glasses," she said. "Besides we've spent so much time that we ought to be starting home for lunch."

It was rather a quiet procession that started down the hill. Miss Dunbar went first. Gerald followed. He was sorry for Miss Dunbar, of course, but very interested to think of the discovery of a deep hole in the mountain.

Talking over his shoulder to Harry, he said, "You know it's not so queer about that hole. All these mountains are made of limestone, Pa says, and limestone is easily worn away by water, and that's why there are so many caves in Lebanon."

Harry did not reply. He was beginning to feel hot, as the sun was right overhead, and he wondered what they were going to have for lunch. Boadie followed along at the end. She was very silent and seemed to be deep in her own thoughts.

Soon they came to the place where the path branched off toward the boys' house. Miss Dunbar waved goodbye and kept right on past. But Boadie hesitated a moment.

"What do you think about tomorrow, boys? You know *you* didn't even get to the Mystery House today."

"We found a mystery though — sort of," said Harry. "*You* didn't find anything."

He was beginning to feel very hungry and a bit cross and he started down the path toward home when something Boadie said made him stop.

"I don't know yet," Boadie was saying slowly. "I saw something in that house that seems queer to me."

"What did you see?" asked Gerald.

"It's one of the windows," replied Boadie. "Did you ever see a window that looks out on — nothing at all?"

Miss Dunbar was calling to Boadie.

"Just tell me what you mean!" demanded Gerald.

"I can't now," said Boadie. "I've got to go. But you know — I'm almost sorry we started exploring that little house." And without another word she was off, running down the path.

3 DANNY'S DISCOVERY

GROWNUPS are so slow, thought Harry. He was sitting on a stool near the living-room door, waiting for a chance to speak to Ma. He wanted to tell her that he and Gerald were going up on the mountain, but he knew it was no use trying to interrupt. Ma had a caller, and the lady's voice went on and on.

I guess there's no hurry anyway, thought Harry resignedly. Gerald still has to finish reading his chapter in the French book.

He knew that Ma had seen him slide into the room and sit down near the door. So now he settled himself to watch Miss Mariam as she talked. She was a small lady, not much taller than Gerald. Harry liked the way her black hair was brushed smoothly back over her ears to a low knot behind. Her lips curved prettily as she talked, mostly in Arabic, but now and then sliding into English which she spoke easily. She had a pleasant way of glancing at him now and then, to include him in the conversation like any other grownup, but Harry didn't pay much attention to what she said. It was something about some disagreeable summer people who had moved into the house next to hers. As she talked, Harry watched her hands, moving all the time, now in a soft slow upward wave, now dropping suddenly in her lap, palms up, and now one forefinger moving slowly back from her knee as she explained something.

Suddenly Harry heard his own name. Miss Mariam was

saying, "And their boy — a bit younger than Harry here — behaves in a terrible manner! And I had so looked forward to having some American children next door to me!"

She turned here and smiled warmly at Harry. "I made some fresh macaroons yesterday. Here they are, for you and Gerald." She picked up a package beside her and handed it to him. Then she added a little ruefully, "I thought that might be one way I could make friends with the new boy next door. But when I handed him one over the wall he threw it out into the road. He said he didn't eat dirty Arab food." She smiled and added sympathetically, "He just doesn't know any better, poor fellow."

Harry was speechless with indignation for a minute. Then he sputtered, "Well he needn't have *wasted* it by grabbing it and throwing it away!"

Miss Mariam laughed and Harry's mother remarked comfortingly, "Well anyway, Miss Mariam knows one place where her macaroons will always be appreciated. . . . Harry, did you want to ask me something?"

"Oh yes," replied Harry. "Gerald and I want to go up and explore the ruined house. Is it O.K.?"

"Of course," said his mother. "Have you finished your studying?"

"I have," rejoined Harry virtuously. "And Gerald is just finishing." He jumped up from his stool and was turning to go when his mother spoke again.

"And Harry — come here a moment."

He went and stood beside his mother. She spoke in a low voice.

"Would you two boys mind taking Danny along this morning? He hasn't gone with you for the last few days, and the ruined house isn't a very long walk."

"Oh Ma!" Harry began to protest. "He's only *five*, and . . ."

A slight gesture from his mother stopped him and he turned to see Danny standing in the door. His white sailor cap was in his hand, and his small knapsack was slung over his shoulders. He did not say a word, but his eyes were hopeful.

Harry turned to his mother and raised his eyebrows. "Sure," he said. "Danny's a good hiker. We'd like to have him along."

With a polite goodbye to Miss Mariam and a warm smile from his mother, he left the room.

"Come on, Danny," he said; "Gel must be about ready now."

They found Gerald in the vineyard, eating a bunch of grapes, the brim of his white canvas hat pulled way down over his eyes to shield them from the sun. He eyed his brothers silently as they approached, pausing now and then to see how far he could spit a grape seed.

"Took you a long time," he finally remarked to Harry.

"I didn't know you were ready," said Harry. "Danny's coming, too."

"O.K.," said Gerald, handing each of the boys a small bunch from his own bunch of grapes. "See if you can hit that rock."

For a minute or two they stood in silence, eating the grapes and spitting the seeds at the rock.

Then Gerald tossed his bunch away and said, "Let's go." Turning to Danny he asked, "Why do you want to lug that knapsack along? It'll be hot, and we'll be back for lunch."

"I don't mind," replied Danny. "It's for my collection. Thought I'd look for some fossils while I'm up there."

"All right," said Gerald. "But you won't find any sharks' teeth or fossil clams up there. They're mostly at the clay mounds."

"I want to take it anyway," said Danny perseveringly.

The three boys started scrambling up the mountain. Gerald led the way, pausing now and then in his long strides so that Danny could catch up, and Harry followed Danny. Danny's face grew very red but he plodded along without stopping, even starting to walk around Gerald once when Gerald had paused.

"Hold on!" said Gerald. "Even if you are a good hiker, you have to stop now and then to get your breath and not waste your strength." Danny stopped, but tossed a stone down the hillside to show that he wasn't really tired.

A moment later, they heard a shout from above. Boadie was dancing around impatiently on the flat terrace where the ruined house stood.

"Come on!" she called. "There's lots to be done if we — " She stopped suddenly, a look of dismay spreading over her face as she caught sight of Danny.

Danny sat down on a little rock by the path, and began examining his dusty shoes with a great show of interest. His ears were very red.

"This is our brother," Gerald called back sternly. "His name is Danny and he's coming with us."

"Oh!" said Boadie reluctantly. "Well, come on then."

The boys soon reached the terrace and moved into the shade of the ruined walls to rest. Gerald couldn't help thinking again to himself that there really wasn't much to explore here.

The house looked like a little square box which some giant had pushed back into the mountainside so that the mountain formed the back wall of the building. However, the giant had pushed one side of the box a little harder than the other, so that the north side was shorter than the south side, and the house looked a little askew. Because of this odd position, the short, northerly side of the house faced back to the mountain, while the long southerly side, with one window in it, looked out over the village below. The front of the house, facing west and slightly north, had a door and a window in it, and it was by this wall that the children were sitting and resting.

"A very sensible way to build this house," remarked Gerald. "See how cool it is; the sun won't get around to this front part until this afternoon."

Nobody replied. Suddenly Gerald inquired, "Where's Miss Dunbar?"

"Up there on the ledge above the house," replied Boadie carelessly.

"No she's not," contradicted Gerald. "We would have seen her as we came up. There's no one on the ledge."

"Well, go and look again," said Boadie calmly. "She's there."

Gerald got up and walked out to the edge of the terrace where he could see over the little house. At first he saw only the clump of pines and the ledge. Then he noticed a long brown figure stretched out at full length on the rock. It was Miss Dunbar, lying flat on her back, her brown straw hat resting on her face.

"What's the matter? Is she asleep?" he asked.

"Oh no," said Boadie. "She's thinking. This is one of her thinking days. Sometimes she lies like that for hours with her hat over her eyes and thinks."

"What's she thinking about?" inquired Danny, who had

climbed up the hill a little way in order to see Miss Dunbar.

"I don't know," said Boadie. "Perhaps about what she's been reading. She generally has a book on the ground beside her."

"It's nice," remarked Danny thoughtfully. "It looks like a comfortable way to think."

Boadie looked at him in surprise. Then turning to the other boys she remarked impatiently, "Oh come on now, you've rested long enough. We must get busy and clear this house out first of all. Look at all the thorns and bushes growing right up in the floor of the house. We can't discover anything till we get it clear."

"Just a minute," said Gerald firmly. "First you tell us what you meant last night when you talked about a window 'that looks out on nothing.' "

"Oh, all right," said Boadie. "Come along."

She led the way across the threshold of the little house, pushing through the thistles and stepping lightly between or over the square stones which lay helter-skelter on the floor, just as they had landed when the roof fell in. It was as bright in here as it was outside, for the sun poured in between the walls that remained standing. Boadie paused in the middle of the house on a little pile of stones and pointed first to the window in the south side.

"Now what do you see out there?" she demanded.

"Oh — the village, and the path, and the sea way off, and — lots of things," said Harry.

"All right," said Boadie. "Now look out of the front window and what do you see?"

Gerald was nearest to it. A little impatiently he replied — "Oh, you can see Beirut way down there, and the plain, and the coastline up to the north — and the road winding

around the mountain toward Souk."

"Now!" said Boadie dramatically. "Just look out of that last window, that one on the north, and what do you see?"

All the children moved over to the last window.

Harry sighed. "Nothing much," he said.

A tall blue thistle swayed gently in the breeze just beyond the window ledge. A few feet away, the side of the mountain rose straight up, a rocky wall which shut out all the view. Some thorny bushes grew out of the cracks of the rock, and a few ferns peeped out where the rock met the ground.

Disappointed, Gerald turned to Boadie. "The window certainly looks out on nothing," said he. "But what's so interesting about that?"

Boadie explained. "Well, what do we have windows for? Aren't they to look out of? Now here's one that doesn't look out on anything. There's something queer about that, and I mean to find out what this window was for."

"Phooey," said Gerald good-naturedly. "It was just so they could get a breeze through the house on a hot day. That's all."

"Then tell me this," said Boadie portentously. "WHY DID THEY MAKE THIS WINDOW BIGGER THAN THE OTHERS?"

Gerald and Harry looked around at the other two windows. It was true. The other two windows were fairly small. But this one, which faced no view at all, was wider and deeper. The ledge was rather low. In fact Danny was leaning on it, resting his elbows on the ledge, his chin cupped in his hands. He had not said a word, but now he spoke meditatively, still staring out of the window.

"This window *doesn't* look out at nothing," said Danny. "I think it's a very interesting window. Look at the ant path there. And there are some pretty crystals showing in the cracks of that rock. Maybe I can break some off and add them to my collection."

In a moment he was climbing out over the ledge and the others saw him squatting down to watch the ants running to and fro on the tiny path they had made in the dirt.

Boadie sighed. "I don't know why," she said, "but it makes me feel sad to look out of this window in the little ruined house."

Finally Gerald remarked, "Well, I can't see that this window is so important even though it is a bit different from the others. But we'll see. Let's get this place cleaned out first."

Immediately the children set to work. With Gerald's pocketknife Boadie began cutting down thistles. Gerald and Harry started moving out some of the stones that littered the ground inside the house. Cautiously they would tip a stone up on its edge and look where it had lain in order to make sure that no scorpion or centipede was hiding underneath. Then if it was not too heavy, they would lift it together and carry it to the edge of the terrace where they would send it rolling and crashing down the mountainside. When they found a larger stone they would heave and push and roll it along to the edge, giving it a final push and then watching it as it bounded down the slope. It was hot work but the children kept at it so hard that they scarcely noticed the time pass. It was surprising how quickly the little house began to look more like a house and less like an abandoned ruin. Boadie had cleared the thistles off a little space outside in front, and she paused to look admiringly at the inside as the boys returned from dumping another stone over the edge.

"You know," she said excitedly, "even if we don't make any discoveries right away, at least we will have this house for our very own to play in."

Suddenly Gerald asked, "Where's Danny?"

They walked to the corner of the house where Danny had been inspecting the ant path, but he was nowhere in sight.

"Danny!" he called.

"I'm up here," came the answer, from the ledge above.

The three children climbed up and found Danny stretched

out on the ledge, not far from Miss Dunbar. Like her, he had his hat over his eyes.

When he heard his brothers' footsteps he sat up and explained, "I got tired down there, so I've been up here thinking, with Miss Dunbar."

At this Miss Dunbar sat up suddenly and looked around, her eyes blinking a little in the bright sunshine.

"Who, may I ask is this?" she inquired, looking at Danny in a puzzled fashion.

"This is my brother Danny," said Gerald.

"How do you do," said Danny gravely.

"I'm very well, thank you," replied Miss Dunbar. "Are you exploring the ruined house, too?"

"No," answered Danny. "I just came along. I'm a collector."

"What do you collect?" inquired Miss Dunbar politely.

"Oh, anything that's interesting," said Danny. "Sometimes beetles or queer-looking plants. But mostly stones. I have a very good collection of stones."

"I should think there would be plenty to collect around here," observed Miss Dunbar.

"There are," said Danny. "But I only keep the good ones."

"How do you know which ones are good?"

"I take them home and ask Pa. If he says, 'Keep that one until you get a better one of the same kind,' it means that it's good."

"I should like to see your collection someday," said Miss Dunbar. Then she turned to the others and said, "It's time to be starting home. Any discoveries in the old house yet?"

The children looked at one another.

"Not yet," said Gerald. "We're getting it cleared out. We'll come back tomorrow and finish."

Miss Dunbar stood up and moved toward the path, while the others followed. Suddenly Gerald looked at Danny.

"What happened to your knapsack?" he asked.

Everybody stopped.

"I'll want it again tomorrow," replied Danny. "So I'm just going to leave it here."

"You can't do that," said Gerald. "Somebody might pick it up. Go and get it."

"Nobody'll see it," said Danny, not budging. "It's in a very good hiding place."

"Hurry up," said Gerald impatiently. "You're keeping us all waiting."

Slowly Danny turned and walked toward the ruined house. He stopped once and looked around pleadingly at his brother.

"It's a *very* safe hiding place," he said.

"Go on," said Gerald sternly. "You can't leave that thing up here. You don't want to lose it, do you? . . . Here, I'll come with you."

Danny's face brightened as his older brother took his hand and accompanied him to the house. The rest of the party sat down patiently beside the path to wait. They saw Danny lead Gerald around the house to the side where the ant path was. Harry examined the scratches on his arms where the thistles had left their mark. His arms and legs ached and he was glad it was nearly time for lunch.

Then a call made him look up.

"Hey kids! Come here quickly! Come and see what Danny has found!" Gerald's voice came from the other side of the ruined house.

"Can I go?" asked Boadie looking quickly at Miss Dunbar.

Miss Dunbar said, "Of course. There's plenty of time."

Quickly Harry and Boadie scrambled over to the terrace, scattering little stones right and left, and ran around the house.

There was no one there! The little ants scurried back and forth along the ant path. The blue thistle by the window ledge swayed in the breeze, and Harry turned to Boadie in baffled amazement.

"Where could they go so fast?"

He and Boadie peered into the little house, but it was empty and still.

A quick whistle behind them made them turn around suddenly, but there was nothing there but the rocky side of the mountain, with a few thistles and bushes waving in the wind. As they stared, suddenly one overhanging bush, growing right out of the rock, waved harder than the others, and Danny's round face peered out at them, smiling broadly. Then he pushed the bush up and crawled right out from the rock itself, and Gerald came crawling out after him.

"It's a little cave!" said Gerald. "Danny found it himself! Come in and look." One by one they crawled in through the low opening covered by the overhanging bush, Boadie going first and Harry following, with Gerald and Danny last. Once inside, they sat down in wonder, in a little circle. It was cool and dark in here after the hot sunshine outside. At first they could see nothing, but as their eyes became accustomed to the darkness, they looked around. The sloping roof of rock went higher as it went back from the opening, high enough for a man to stand up in one place. The whole cave was only about ten feet square, roughly speaking, but it was very irregular in shape. Little ferns grew around the opening and there was a damp, sweet smell in here, very different from the hot dry air outside. On a little shelf of rock by the entrance reposed Danny's knapsack.

"It's a lovely place!" exclaimed Boadie. "How lucky that you brought Danny today. How did you ever find it?" she asked admiringly.

Danny tried hard not to look pleased, but his ears grew red as he replied: "I just followed the ant path. It went straight to the rock. I knew ants couldn't go through a rock, and I didn't see any of them going up on it, so when the path went under the bush I went there too and I found this. Their hole is just inside the cave — you're spoiling it, Gerald," he ended reproachfully.

Gerald jumped up quickly and began brushing ants off his trousers.

"It seems quite light in here after a little while," remarked Harry, who had straightened up and was standing in the middle of the cave. "Look! There's a little crack up there where the light comes in from above!"

The others looked where Harry was pointing. Sure enough, a small crack of light showed above. A dim beam of light from this crack fell on the soft earth which formed the floor of the little cave. Suddenly Harry gave a shout and pointed at an object lying on the floor.

Boadie gave a chuckle as she went over to pick it up.

"Dunbar's eyeglasses!" she murmured. "My word! I can't wait to see her face when we give them to her. By the way, she must be wondering where we are."

The children looked at one another guiltily.

"I had forgotten about her," said Gerald. "There's something I wanted to — " But he stopped.

"Wanted to what?" asked Harry.

"Never mind now," said Gerald. "If we don't get home promptly we might not be able to come back tomorrow." He crawled through the opening, and the others followed, blinking as they emerged into the sunlight. Once outside, Gerald stopped them.

"Don't you think Danny should give the glasses to Miss Dunbar? He really showed us the way."

"Of course," replied Boadie promptly. "Here you are, Danny." She handed them over, and Danny proudly took them and led the way around the little house.

Miss Dunbar did not seem to have missed the children. She appeared to be thinking again, sitting up against the rock, with her hat pulled down over her eyes. As the children approached she turned around with a little start. Danny came forward and presented the glasses case to her. She stared at it, and then at him, with amazement and delight.

"How did you manage it?" she exclaimed.

All the children tried to explain at once, and gradually Miss Dunbar learned what had happened. As the explanations died down, Gerald noticed that Danny was looking a little downcast.

"What's the matter, Danny?" he asked.

"Well — " said Danny, hesitating. "I did think it was a

good hiding place. Now it's not a secret. Everybody knows about it."

Miss Dunbar spoke quickly. "Certainly it's a secret. Nobody here is going to tell about it. Are we?" she inquired severely, looking around at Boadie, Gerald and Harry in turn.

"No!" they chorused.

"Not unless Danny gives us permission first," added Gerald.

"Only my father and my mother," said Danny solemnly. "I'll tell them."

Looking cheerful again he started down the hill, and everyone followed. Gerald and Harry came last, and once Gerald paused and said in a low tone to Harry, "All the same, I think Danny's not the first person to have been in that cave."

"Why?" asked Harry looking at him quickly.

"I'm not sure," said Gerald. "But I saw something there that makes me think so. Tomorrow I'm going to bring a flashlight with me and examine that place carefully."

Not another word would he say, and the procession went down the hill in silence, each person thinking his own thoughts.

THE MIDDLE of the day was always a very quiet, restful time in Shemlan. The hot sun was straight overhead. Gerald and Harry's parents were having siestas, and for an hour or two the boys were expected to take life easily. This was not the time of day for exploring. It was better to stretch out in the cool shade of the big oak tree by the house and play parcheesi or read the Jungle Books. Few sounds came up from the village below; everything seemed to be sleeping under the summer sun. As the shadows grew longer, though, the boys began to stir around. Then came the sound of the teacups being set out on the back porch. Gerald yawned comfortably and sitting up in the canvas deck chair, remarked to Harry, "I wonder what's up for this afternoon."

This stretch between tea and supper was usually the best part of the day. Pa and Ma were free then; there would be tennis, or baseball; or perhaps a hike to the fossil clams; or an excursion to Heatherstone, with a picnic supper

So the family gathering at tea on the back porch was always important; plans for the afternoon would be unfolded. Today when Harry and Gerald arrived at the back porch their mother was already pouring the tea from the shining brown teapot. Pa was sitting relaxed on the stone bench across from her, his legs, in white duck tennis pants, stretched out luxuriously in front of him. His teacup was resting on the bench beside him, and he stirred the tea thoughtfully. Danny and the youngest son John, seated side by side next to their father, were engaged in diligently biting the rims of their gingersnaps into an interesting scalloped pattern. They were working silently, eying each other's progress, and hardly noticed the arrival of their older brothers. It was a comfortable and usual scene, and there seemed to be no reason for the somewhat troubled expression on Ma's face, or the silence which fell as the boys came up.

But she poured the boys' tea, and at Gerald's inquiry, "What are we doing this afternoon?" she looked at Pa.

"Well," said Pa, tasting his tea with relish and helping himself to a couple of gingersnaps, "it seems that you boys have become involved in a social obligation."

Harry looked solemn. This didn't sound very interesting.

"It seems there's a boy just arrived in the village — an American boy about your age." The boys' faces brightened. "And his mother has asked your mother if she would bring you to call this afternoon."

"Good!" said Gerald.

"Well, we'll see about that," remarked his father coolly. "According to reports, this boy isn't very well behaved. But maybe he's all right. Anyway you boys know how to behave — most of the time. We'll expect you to behave this afternoon."

"And Danny, and me?" asked John. "Can we go?"

"You stay with me," said Pa. "We'll do something else."

"When can we go?" asked Gerald.

"Right after tea?" asked Harry hopefully.

"Yes, as soon as you're finished. We might as well go and

do the right thing," said their mother without enthusiasm.

"Go along and enjoy yourselves," said Pa. "I shall have another cup of tea."

It was rather warm walking along the dusty road toward the house just beyond Miss Mariam's little cottage. As they passed Miss Mariam's the boys looked down, but she was not in sight. Probably she was having tea under the huge oak tree on the other side of her house. They almost wished they could go down and join her; she might have some more of those macaroons, and her outdoor room under the deep shade of the oak tree was always inviting.

As Harry looked down at the little house he had a disturbing thought. What was it that this new boy had said to Miss Mariam? Something about the cookies being dirty, and he had thrown them in the road? Well, maybe he just didn't know any better; maybe he was really afraid of Arabs. Harry began to feel hopeful again; American boys were rare around here.

He had lagged behind a little as he was thinking these thoughts; Gerald and his mother were already stopping in front of the big wooden door of the house. He caught up with them as his mother lowered her parasol and knocked on the door.

"What's his name?" asked Gerald urgently, in a last-minute rush.

"Edmund," replied his mother. "Edmund Bixton."

"Eddie," whispered Harry to himself. "Sounds good."

The door swung open wide suddenly, but there seemed to be no one there. A cool narrow hallway stretched before them, leading into a living room beyond.

"I wonder — " said Ma hesitatingly. "Perhaps I'd better knock again."

A loud "*Boo!*" made them all jump, as a boy nearly as tall as Harry leaped out from behind the door.

"Boy, did you look funny!" he chuckled.

For a second the boys' mother looked at him in amazement; then she smiled politely and held out her hand.

"Edmund?" she said. "I am Mrs. Sawyer and these are my boys, Harry and Gerald."

"How did you know who I was?" demanded Edmund, backing off with his hands behind his back. His narrow blue eyes looked warily at Ma. Harry wondered how a boy so big could look so babyish. Though he was tall, his face was round and soft looking, and his hair instead of being cut short for the hot summer days was long behind the ears, and a long floppy piece of it hung down over his forehead.

At this moment a lady came hurrying down the little hallway. She was tall and slim, but her dark eyes seemed troubled as she came toward them.

"Edmund dear! That's no way to welcome our visitors!" She put her hand out to the boys' mother. "This is lovely of you to come. I'm afraid Edmund was so excited over having some boys to play with that he forgot his manners."

"Who's excited?" muttered Edmund.

His mother continued, paying no attention to him, "And this is Gerald? and Harry? Now come right in and cool off in here." She led the way on into the living room.

"She's nice," thought Harry to himself. He liked the way her dark hair waved softly up to the top of her head, and he liked her thin green summer dress and the cool smell of cologne that trailed after her as he followed the rest of them into the room.

As in all the Arab houses, the living room here was the center of the house. Only the western end of it opened with big arched windows out over the mountains and sea. The sea blazed and glittered in the afternoon sun, but the room inside was filled with a cool green light because of a large awning that shaded the windows. A little tea table was set in one corner. Sandwiches caught the boys' eyes; and a plate of pink-frosted cupcakes. Before anyone else had sat down, Edmund had settled himself in a large wicker armchair next to the tea table and reached for a cake.

"Edmund!" said his mother softly. Edmund settled himself more comfortably and took a large bite out of the cake.

"Mrs. Sawyer, won't you sit here beside me?" said Mrs. Bixton, and the two mothers settled themselves on a little settee at the other side of the table. Harry found a small footstool conveniently near, but he noticed that Gerald remained standing near the door. He seemed to be listening for something.

"Won't you sit down, Gerald?" invited Mrs. Bixton. Gerald came to life and moved over. To everyone's surprise Edmund hopped up and quickly offered him his chair.

"I can sit on the floor over here, on a pillow," he said cheerfully.

Gerald eyed him warily a moment and then instead of taking the offered chair, he bent over it and examined the cushion carefully.

"Gerald!" said his mother.

"Yes, Ma," said Gerald politely, without turning around. Then he put out his hand and gingerly picked up a small round thistle head that had been dropped into the middle of the pillow.

"Sissy!" muttered Edmund.

"My dear, I don't know *what* to say," began Mrs. Bixton apologetically.

Mrs. Sawyer interrupted her.

"Oh never mind," she said. "Now tell me how you like our village. When did you arrive?" The talk began to flow around over Harry's head, while he concentrated on the refreshments. The cupcakes were a disappointment; after the first bite he found they had a funny sort of flavor in them, like perfume. Being hungry he finished his, but he wondered why other people's cakes never tasted as good as the ones at home. He looked over at Gerald to see if he had eaten his cake. Gerald still held half of his in one hand; the fingers of his other hand were idly rolling the little thistle head around and around on the arm of his chair. Once in a while he stopped and again seemed to have that listening look which he had had before — as if he were listening for some other sound, outside the voices of the ladies. Harry decided to listen, too. Soon he did hear an odd little sound; it seemed like a baby crying — a little whimper or two, then silence. Then another whimper.

"Have you a baby in the house?" asked their mother suddenly, when a whimper came, louder than ever, in a pause of the conversation.

"Oh no," replied Mrs. Bixton smiling. "That must be Bouncy. Edmund, you'd better see what's the matter with him. He sounds as if he needs something."

"He's all right," said Edmund lazily, his mouth full of cake. "He's always crying like that."

"Bouncy is Edmund's new puppy," explained Mrs. Bixton turning to the boys. "Why don't you take the boys out and let them see him?" she suggested.

"They don't want to see him," growled Edmund, not moving.

Gerald stood up.

"Yes we do," he said. "If you don't want to show him to us, we can find the way ourselves. He sounds as if he needs something. Come on, Harry."

Edmund, a little surprised, grudgingly stood up and led the way out through a door which took them into the kitchen and out on a terrace behind the house. The whining suddenly ceased when they appeared. As the boys' eyes grew accustomed to the glare of the sunshine they saw a small black and white puppy lying on his stomach, his paws stretched out in front of him. Around his neck was a collar, and a string attached to this was tied to a rock behind him. The little fellow had gone as far as the string would let him and was lying there panting in the hot sun. Just a few inches away, out of his reach, the shadow of the house made a cool shelter, and in this cool spot, Gerald and Harry noticed a pan of water. Gerald turned to Edmund angrily.

"What a dope! Can't you see you've tied him up just where he can't get to his water? Go bring that rock over so he can be in the shade. He's thirsty."

Edmund just stood and looked at the puppy.

"Sure he's thirsty. It serves him right. He needs to be punished."

"What did he do?" inquired Harry.

"Aw, he's always doing things. Chewed up a rubber ball of mine yesterday."

"And you think you're punishing him for *that?*" demanded Gerald. "In the first place, he can't remember that far back. And in the second place, for a puppy it isn't wrong. He needs to chew on things and you probably didn't give him anything to use his teeth on. Now let him off that string or I'll do it myself."

As Edmund did not move, Gerald walked over to the

puppy. When he approached, the puppy rolled his eyes up at him and shrank away in fear. Gerald spoke softly to him.

"All right, boy. Good dog, come here, boy." Carefully he untied the string from the collar and lifted the trembling puppy in his hands, talking softly to him all the time. Then he set him down in the shade by the pan of water. The puppy crouched down there trembling, but did not try to touch the water. Gerald continued talking to him softly, gently stroking his head with two fingers. Then he dipped a finger into the water and touched the puppy's nose with it. The puppy shook his head and looked up at Gerald. Then at last he dipped his head down and began to lap up the water. Gerald stood back a little and the three boys watched in silence. For a long time the little pup stood there and drank and drank, his little sides trembling and swelling. Finally he stopped and looked around. For the first time his tail came up and moved once. Then he took a step toward Gerald. Gerald again spoke to him softly, not moving. The puppy came nearer and nearer; finally he stopped at Gerald's feet and began sniffing them. Again the tail came up and moved. Gerald squatted down and patted him again. Harry joined him, while Edmund stood looking on in disdain.

"Whatever made you call him Bouncy?" asked Harry. "I never saw a quieter puppy."

"It wasn't my idea," said Edmund. "Mother named him. He was much more lively when he came. Much *too* lively. I've calmed him down. He's got to learn not to be a nuisance."

"You don't seem to know much about dogs," said Gerald. "You've got this one scared to death. Don't you *like* him?"

"Not much," said Edmund.

"We'll take him if you want," said Harry eagerly. "Give him to us."

Edmund's chin went up obstinately.

"Oh no!" said he. "He's my property. You can't have him."

"But if you don't *like* him — " began Harry.

"That's got nothing to do with it," replied Edmund sullenly. "He's mine and you can't have him. I *don't* like him, but he's my property and that's that. I'll do what I want with him, so give him back to me and let me tie him up. He's got to suffer for being a nuisance."

He reached out and grabbed the puppy roughly to jerk him out of Gerald's hands. Harry gave him a quick, hard poke in the ribs under his arm, which made him drop his hands and yell.

"Mother! Mother!" he yelled. He stood there with his mouth wide open, and to the boys' amazement the tears began rolling down his cheeks as he roared.

"Mother! They hit me!" He turned and went into the house, crying and yelling.

Harry turned in horror to Gerald.

"Gosh, I only poked him! Do you suppose I've really done something to him?"

"Naw," said Gerald reassuringly. "He's just a big baby. You've never met one like him before, that's all."

"Here, fellow," he continued turning to the puppy, "we'll tie you up again over here in the shade." He walked over to the rock and carried it back near the pan of water; tied the string to the puppy's collar and stood back to look at him. The pup thumped his tail once, then curled up in the shade and went fast asleep.

By this time the yells in the house had subsided.

"We'd better go back in," said Gerald, and he started into the house, Harry following him reluctantly.

The group in the living room was rather silent as they reentered. Edmund, still sniffing loudly now and then, was seated again in the big chair next to the tea table, stuffing another cake into his mouth with an injured air. Gerald and Harry looked at their mother, who raised her eyebrows questioningly. Harry looked down at the rug and apologized to it briefly.

"Sorry. I didn't mean to hurt you."

Neither the rug nor Edmund responded. Mrs. Bixton spoke reassuringly.

"I'm sure you didn't. You must excuse Edmund if he seems to get upset too easily. You see, he's been sick such a lot."

Watching Edmund stuff himself with cake, Gerald muttered, "And no wonder!" Harry heard him and felt a little better, but Mrs. Bixton had turned to their mother.

"Poor boy, he does find it hard to find anything to *do* around here. He has no playmates, and there's nothing to see except the wild mountainsides and the quiet village. What do *you* boys find to do with yourselves I wonder?" she asked turning to Harry.

"*Here?* In *Shemlan?*" asked Harry wondering where to begin. "Well, yesterday we were up on the mountain with Boadie (she's an English girl) — "

"Playing with a little *girl!*" interrupted Edmund scornfully. "An *English* one! What babies!"

Harry eyed him wrathfully, but continued in a temperate tone: "You don't know what she's like. Every time we meet her, something interesting happens. Yesterday we found — ow!" He rubbed his ankle where Gerald had kicked him hard. Edmund was leaning forward with sharp interest in his eye.

"You found what?"

"Oh — " Harry hesitated. "We found some glasses that her governess had lost," he finished lamely.

"That's *not* what you were going to say!" exclaimed Edmund. "You found something else up there on the mountain. What was it?"

Harry did not answer.

"Edmund dear, never mind. Perhaps another day you can go exploring on the mountain with the boys." His mother looked pleadingly at him.

But Edmund was not to be stopped.

"Never mind, Edmund dear," he mimicked. "*I* don't mind. I'll find out for myself what their secret is if they don't want to tell me. They and the *sweet* little English girl they play with."

"Oh dear, it's nearly six o'clock!" exclaimed Mrs. Sawyer looking at the clock. "We must be going right away."

Gerald and Harry jumped up with alacrity. They went to the door and waited impatiently while their mother picked up her parasol and said goodbye. Edmund sidled over to them and remarked again in an undertone, "You just wait! I have my ways of finding things out!"

"Oh phooey," said Gerald quietly. These friendly farewells having been made, the boys said a more conventional goodbye to their hostess, and followed their mother out to the road.

"Gee, what a relief to be out of there," sighed Gerald.

"Was he pretty awful?" inquired their mother sympathetically.

"He's a pain," said Harry.

Supper was over, and the family was on the balcony watching the last glow of daylight over the sea. One star gleamed brightly above the horizon.

"Pa," said Gerald suddenly. "Isn't there any way we can

get that puppy away from him? The puppy'll die if he goes on being treated like that!"

"I don't see how, son." His father's tone was thoughtful. "There are no laws here about the mistreatment of animals. The only thing we could do is to persuade his mother to give us the puppy."

"She won't," broke in Harry gloomily. "All he has to do is yell, and he gets what he wants." He repeated the story of this afternoon's incident, and wound up, "So there he was, crying like a baby for nothing — and getting stuffed with cake as a reward."

Danny, who had been leaning against the iron balustrade looking out to the sea through the bars, now turned around and showed that he had been listening with interest.

"You mean if he cries hard enough his mother gives him anything?" For a moment he glanced at his own mother sitting on a little rocking chair near him — then turned his eyes back to Harry.

"That's right," said Harry. "But don't you try it on Ma, because it won't work."

Everybody laughed except Danny, who turned around and began looking at the sea again.

"I know," he said thoughtfully.

The light faded slowly from the sky. Gerald's and Harry's thoughts were gloomy. Presently their mother said, "Time for bed, Danny and John."

A sleepy figure uncurled from her lap and slid to the floor, walked over and stood by Danny.

Taking John's hand, Danny turned around and asked Gerald, "Are we going to the ruined house tomorrow morning — and to my secret cave?"

"You bet," said Gerald cheerfully.

"Good night everybody." But as Danny went contentedly into the house with John, Gerald did not feel as cheerful as he had sounded. He could not help wondering if un-
friendly eyes would discover Danny's secret.

5 BOADIE MEETS THE ENEMY

A COUNCIL OF WAR was being held on the ledge above the old ruined house.

"What a villain!" exclaimed Boadie. "The big hulking bully!"

"And you should have heard what he said about you, Boadie!" said Gerald chuckling.

"Me?" said Boadie. "He doesn't know me."

"I'll say he doesn't," agreed Gerald with fervor. "But when Harry told him we had been playing with you, he said we were sissies to play with a 'sweet little English girl.'"

Boadie's pigtails quivered with fury.

"I'll jolly well show him!" she exploded. "I'll sweet-little-English-girl him! Oh!" she sputtered. "I can't wait to meet him!"

"I hope I'm around when you do," said Gerald. "But the real question is — what can we do about that puppy?"

Boadie had no doubts about what ought to be done.

"We've got to steal him. We've got to rescue him fast."

"We should be able to but we can't," said Gerald. "It happens to be against the law."

"Oh, phooey on the law!" (Boadie was picking up American expressions fast.) "The law should prevent people like that from owning poor helpless animals. If you boys are scared of stealing that little pup, leave it to me. I'll save him."

"Don't be silly," said Gerald severely. "We're not *scared;*

it's wrong, that's all. Besides," he added practically, "you'd be found out right away. You can't hide a dog forever in a little village like this."

At this point Danny rose to the surface with a suggestion.

"Maybe the little dog'll run away by himself," he remarked helpfully. "That wouldn't be stealing, would it? If he did it by himself?"

Gerald smiled at Danny. "He's too little and much too scared to think of that," he explained.

But Boadie was staring at Danny with a speculative eye.

"Danny, you've got a lot of ideas for a small head," she said with approval. Then suddenly changing the subject she said, "Now what's the next step in exploring the little house?"

"First, I suppose," said Gerald glumly, "we'll have to post a guard. We'll have to take turns watching out that that Edmund doesn't come along and discover everything."

To his surprise, Boadie eagerly volunteered.

"Danny and I'll stand guard," she offered. "He can be looking for fossils and crystals for his collection up on the ledge, and I'll get him to explain the fossils to me."

Gerald looked at her a little suspiciously, wondering what she was up to. But Boadie's face was all innocence.

"Dunbar was giving me a lecture yesterday about the fossils. She said Danny could show me some samples."

Automatically their eyes turned up the hill to where Miss Dunbar sat on a campstool, sketching. The restored eyeglasses were on, and her hat was pulled down low over her eyes. She sat very straight and only her hand moved as she worked at the drawing. In her brown dress and hat, sitting so still, she looked almost like one of the rocks on the mountain, Danny thought.

Though most of the rocks are gray, he thought to himself. She's more the color of a fossil shark's tooth — smooth and brown.

Gerald's voice brought him back to his surroundings.

"Well, all right," he was saying. "If you and Danny keep watch, Harry and I'll go over the cave carefully to see if there's anything interesting. I brought along a flashlight today."

"We'll be just above you on the ledge," said Boadie. "Just yell at us through the hole if you find anything."

As Harry crawled into the dark coolness of the little cave after Gerald, he inquired, "Now will you show me what it is you thought was so interesting?"

"It may not be much," replied Gerald. "Over here in the back corner," he said moving the flashlight's beam. "It looked to me like pottery — yes, it is, a broken water jar."

"Is it ancient, do you think?" asked Harry. "Roman or something?"

"I doubt it," said Gerald. "Here — hold the flashlight a minute. Look — the pieces go together quite easily. It's just an ordinary pottery water jar with a spout. But you see, it shows someone besides ourselves has inhabited this cave."

Harry glanced around at the opening a little nervously.

"Not *recently*," said Gerald. "This broken pottery is all cobwebby — and don't forget that that little house has been in ruins for years and years — ever since we can remember, in fact. I wish we could find something more interesting than this water jar, though," he ended. "Here — let's have the flashlight again. We'll do this scientifically."

He moved back to the opening of the cave and began a steady, careful scrutiny of the wall of the cave, moving along very slowly.

"You watch too, Harry," he instructed. "You might see something that I missed."

"But what am I supposed to be looking for?" asked Harry.

"*Anything*," said Gerald. "Anything that seems unusual or odd. Especially anything that might be a sign of someone's having been here before."

In silence the search continued. One beam of light shone dimly through the hole in the ceiling above them, and down through the hole came the murmur of voices. Mostly the murmur of one voice.

"I thought Danny was supposed to be lecturing on fossils to Boadie. Sounds to me as if Boadie was doing most of the talking," commented Harry.

Gerald did not reply. Patiently and painstakingly he was examining every inch of the cave wall. As he came around again toward the opening, from which he had started, he stopped a minute and stretched.

"Well," he said, "it's disappointing. There are some nice crystals here and there on the rock, but I'd hoped there'd be something more recent." He glanced over at the water jar. "But that still shows that someone has been in this cave, and I don't mean the cavemen."

At this moment a little stone came rattling down through the hole above and fell on the cave floor. Then the beam of light was darkened and Boadie's voice came down through the hole.

"The enemy's approaching! — I think. Boy about your size, Harry — wearing those American pantaloons. Stay where you are."

Gerald and Harry quietly moved over to the opening of the cave and peered through the bush that hung over it. Sure enough they could hear footsteps coming up the mountain, but the climber was already on the other side of the ruined house and climbing up to the ledge. So the boys moved back till they were standing directly under the hole.

"Oh boy, this ought to be good!" said Gerald. "Now listen to Boadie lay into him."

The first voice they heard was Edmund's.

"Hey! Have you seen a couple of boys around here?"

Then as the boys waited breathlessly for the blast, a silky-sweet voice replied, a voice which they scarcely recognized as Boadie's.

"Pardon me? Oh, what a fright you gave me! Boys? Why yes, here's a boy. This is Danny, a little friend of mine."

No sound from Danny, but the tone of Edmund's reply was contemptuous.

"I'm not looking for a *baby*. I mean *boys*. Around my age. Were they here today?"

"Oh, you mean *big* boys!" How could Boadie's voice sound so admiring? "It seems to me there *were* some big rough things around here earlier, but they seem to have disappeared off the face of the earth. They weren't interested in seeing me do my pretty embroidery." Her tone quivered. "And just see where I pricked my finger with the needle this morning."

Edmund's voice was unsympathetic.

"I don't see anything."

"Well, of course you don't understand how a girl feels. All you boys care about is things like those old Turkish trenches, and playing soldiers."

"What trenches? Where?" demanded Edmund.

"Oh, around on the next shoulder of the hill," said Boadie. "The Turks dug the trenches during the war, but they never used them. If you don't find those boys there now, they'll probably be there this afternoon. They and their wild games!"

Harry clapped his hand over his mouth, but it was too late — a muffled sound from the inside of the mountain reached the ears of the three on the ledge.

"What was that?" demanded Edmund.

"Oh dear! What was it?" asked Boadie.

"Mice?" suggested Danny helpfully.

Edmund stood up and looked around.

"Who's that woman up there?" he asked.

"Sh! That's my governess," replied Boadie.

"Well *she* couldn't have made that noise. It sounded as if it came from right under our feet." He shuddered a little. "Almost *human*."

"Oh I wouldn't say *that*," said Boadie. "Unless you're superstitious. That old ruined house down there — sometimes there are queer stories about noises around old deserted houses like that."

"You mean they say that house is *haunted*?" asked Edmund. "I don't believe in that stuff!"

"Of course not," replied Boadie reassuringly. "Neither do I. But what a weird sound it was. — I wonder," she continued in a meditative way, "do you suppose this mountain could be an old volcano? Sometimes they quiet down for years and people think they're extinct; and then they start to rumble and come alive."

There was silence for a moment or two.

Then Edmund said, a little nervously, "Why don't you ask your governess if she heard anything?"

"I'd rather not," said Boadie. "You ask her."

Edmund looked with exasperation at the timid girl, then he cleared his throat, and called up to Miss Dunbar.

"Hey!"

There was no reply. Miss Dunbar might have turned into a fossil, she was so quiet. Edmund turned to Boadie, who was having trouble keeping a straight face. "What's the matter with her?" he demanded. "Is she deaf?"

"Oh dear no," said Boadie. "It's just that she doesn't always understand these American expressions. In England we say 'Good Morning' instead of 'Hey!' She probably just thought you sneezed."

Another muffled sound came from under their feet.

Edmund jumped back a little, and Boadie looked terrified.

"Let's get out of here," said Edmund quickly turning around and scrambling along the hillside toward the little path. Boadie started after him.

"You know what?" she said, panting along behind him. "It might not be volcanic at all. It might just be the beginning of a little landslide. Sometimes they do have those in these mountains! — Oh dear!" she said, stopping. She raised her voice a little, for Edmund was getting far ahead of her in his hurry to get down the path. "I can't run off like this and leave Miss Dunbar. I'll have to run back up instead of down!" She yelled even louder at the retreating Edmund. "And oh my! we've left little Danny alone on that dangerous spot!"

Edmund did not slow up or even look around. His voice came back over his shoulder: "If he's too dumb to move away, let him stay there!"

Boadie turned away from the hurrying figure and started back toward the ruined house. She called up, "All sereno!"

and two figures popped out of the little house.

"The hero has left!" she announced. "What a man!"

As she arrived on the terrace she remarked, "I thought you were in the cave!"

"We were," answered Gerald. "It was just faster to pop through the window and come through the house than to go around. What a time you gave him!"

"Oh, what a perfect little lady you were!" exclaimed Harry joyously. "I'd never know it was you!"

"I *can* be a lady too!" said Boadie wrathfully, picking up a long-stemmed thistle and starting after Harry in pursuit.

"Oh yes — excuse me — I apologize! Of *course* you're a

lady!" said Harry hastily, dodging the thistle. Boadie forgivingly tossed the thistle over the terrace, and began a little war dance of triumph.

"I chased him off!" she sang. "Single-handed! Ghosts, maybe, I told him! Volcano, maybe! Landslide!"

A little rattle of stones interrupted her chant. The three children stood frozen, listening. Then Danny's head appeared around the corner of the house.

"He said I was a baby!" he stated solemnly.

"Come here, Danny-boy," said Boadie. "You're no baby. You're twice the man *he* is. What a boy! Danny knew how to keep still and not give us away!"

She slapped him on the back and Harry ruffled his hair. Gerald said quietly, "Good boy!" and Danny smiled.

Presently Gerald turned to Boadie and said reproachfully, "You didn't need to tell him we'd be at the Turkish trenches this afternoon! Now I suppose we'll have to go, and we were going to play some tennis."

"Of course you must go or he'll think I just made it up," said Boadie unabashed. "It's a splendid idea; don't you see? Now he'll change his hunting ground to over there!"

Gerald and Harry looked glumly at each other. The idea was good, but the afternoon's plans weren't very enticing. Before they had time to grumble about it, Miss Dunbar's voice came down the hill: "Dorothy! Time to start for home."

In a moment she appeared near them on the path.

"*Who*," she demanded, "was that extraordinary boy? For a moment I thought you were going to bring him up and introduce him to me — and the next instant he was running into the distance as fast as possible. Did someone bite him?"

And she looked severely around at the circle of man-eaters before her.

The four of them began to laugh, and Boadie said, "It's a long story. We'll tell you as we go down the hill."

So as they clambered down Boadie gave the explanation, with corrections and supplements from the boys, interrupted by chuckles as the story came to an end.

Miss Dunbar chuckled too, but she listened without comment to the conclusion. Then she remarked briefly, "I'm sorry for the boy."

"You mean the puppy, don't you?" corrected Harry.

"The puppy too," said Miss Dunbar. "But that boy needs help."

"I did my best," said Boadie modestly, and the boys burst into laughter as they waved goodbye at the fork in the path.

The boys stretched the siesta hour as far as it would go. As a rule they hurried to tea, eager for the afternoon's events. But today they were in no rush.

"What shall we do at the trenches?" asked Harry.

"Oh, I don't know," sighed Gerald. "All we have to do is hang around until he sees us there. Then he'll think it's our secret, I suppose." They were putting away the parcheesi game as they talked, and now they walked out to the back porch, where the cheerful clatter of teacups led them.

Their eyes brightened as they stepped out the door. Ma was pouring tea for a visitor.

"Boadie!" exclaimed Harry. "Did you come to go with us to the trenches?"

Boadie smiled primly as she accepted a cup from their mother.

"I came to have tea with your mother," she replied. "No, I don't think I'd better go to the trenches with you. You forget how frightened I am of rough games." Again she smiled exasperatingly at them as she stirred her tea.

"So you came to make sure *we'd* go. *Slave-driver!*" said Gerald, reaching for a pair of sand tarts.

"Not at all," said Boadie. "I came to ask your mother if she would let Danny come for a walk with me."

"Don't do it, Ma," said Gerald. "She's up to no good. She's a very irresponsible girl."

Boadie looked at Ma with a little shrug as if to say, What can you do?

Ma smiled and said, "Gerald, you'd better pass the sand tarts and try to remember you are the host here. Of course Danny can go with Dorothy if he wants to."

"By the way," said Boadie, changing the subject, "did you find anything in the cave?"

Gerald told her about the pottery jar.

"But that was all," he concluded. "Ma," he said suddenly turning to his mother, "Do you happen to know who used to live in that ruined house of ours?"

"Now let me see," said his mother. "It seems to me that when we first came to Shemlan years ago I asked about it. It looked then just the same as it does now."

Why were grownups always so slow, wondered Harry impatiently.

"But who lived in it before?" he asked urgently.

His mother frowned a little as she looked thoughtfully up at the mountain.

"I'm trying to remember. It seems to me that an old

woman lived there alone. I have the impression that the village thought she was a little crazy. But it was very long ago. She must have been a little odd to live up there all alone."

The children looked up at the mountainside to the little house. From here it looked like a little toy house, with the open door and window facing them.

"How do you suppose she got water up there?" asked Gerald.

"Most of these little houses have cisterns," said Ma. "The rain water would run off the roof and collect in the cistern. She wouldn't need much water, living alone like that."

"Can't you remember *anything* more about her?" urged Gerald.

His mother shook her head. "You could ask Miss Mariam about her sometime. She grew up in Shemlan, and she may remember more about her."

The boys looked at each other. But Boadie seemed to have lost interest in the conversation. She was staring in a puzzled fashion at a large clump of grapevines a few feet away from the porch. Gerald and Harry noticed her expression and followed her gaze. It was an oddly animated grapevine, moving slightly now and then. But what fixed Boadie's fascinated attention was a pair of small scuffed sandals which were planted firmly on the ground under the vine.

Boadie turned and looked inquiringly at the boys beside her. Harry answered her unspoken question in an undertone.

"It's my brother John. He's shy. Just don't pay any attention to him."

"*Another* brother?"

"He's the smallest of us," replied Harry. "He's three. He's very friendly after you know him, but you mustn't run up and kiss him or anything."

"I should hope not!" said Boadie indignantly. Then in a louder tone she added, "It just so happens that I have a little matchbox in my pocket. It's good to keep small things in, like a marble or two, or an acorn. Maybe you'd give it to your brother John for me."

She laid it on the tea table, and set her cup and saucer down near it. One shoe under the grapevine rose and scratched a small brown ankle above the other shoe; then it returned to its original position. Boadie smiled at the grapevine.

"I'll leave the little box here. Thank you for the tea, Mrs. Sawyer. Do you think I could find Danny now and ask him to come with me?"

"I'm here," said a voice.

Boadie looked behind her in surprise, and peered over the back of the stone seat. Danny was squatted down there beside the end of the drainpipe which came down from the roof and ended just above the flower bed beside the porch.

"Are you feeling shy too?" she asked.

Danny stood up and finished the sand tart he was eating.

"No. I was watching a spider spin his web over the drainpipe. He's pretty slow, though, and I've finished my cooky so I can go."

A small blond head poked cautiously out through the grapevine.

"Come along, Danny," said Boadie turning away.

John ran over and sat close to his mother.

"Nobody saw me!" he whispered delightedly. His little

brown hand reached out eagerly and grasped the match-box.

"Where are you going?" called Gerald as Boadie and Danny were disappearing around the corner of the house.

"*Not* to the Turkish trenches," replied Boadie over her shoulder.

Boadie could be very annoying sometimes, thought Gerald.

Τ HE HOTTEST PART of the day was past, but down on the shadeless road the slanting sunlight was still warm on Boadie and Danny. And yet the cool sea breeze blowing up from below made it pleasant walking along the road. Danny carefully stepped along near the edge where the white dust lay thickest, and watched the dust puff out on both sides of his shoes as he walked. Only half his thoughts were on the dust; the other half were occupied with the project in hand.

"Do you know the right way to make friends with a puppy?" he asked Boadie a little anxiously.

"Yes — it's not hard," replied Boadie confidently. "Most puppies want to be friends anyway."

"Are you sure Edmund won't see us?"

Boadie smiled a little complacently. "Things have been arranged, don't you remember?" she said grandly. "Edmund is going to be somewhere else — if I know Edmund. This seems like a good afternoon to get acquainted with his puppy. As a matter of fact," she added, with a deep sigh of satisfaction, "it's a lovely afternoon!"

She looked up at Crystal Mountain on her left, with the long afternoon sunlight shining on its rocks high above them, and on the stony terraces reaching down like steps to the road where they walked. Then she looked to her right, blinking a little in the sun, and saw the houses of the village below her, sloping away to the valleys and the sea; red-tiled roofs and flat roofs of square houses; arched windows and little stone balconies, with grape arbors and flower boxes. Just now they were passing a path which led down, by wide stone steps, to a little flat-roofed cottage. The back of the cottage was built into the slope below them, and the flat roof was no higher than the road on which they were walking. An enormous oak tree at the far corner of the cottage cast a deep shade over the roof, and the size of it made the little house look like a toy.

"What a sweet little cottage under that enormous tree!" exclaimed Boadie.

"That's where Miss Mariam lives," said Danny.

"Then the next house must be Edmund's. Let's peep over that stone wall and see if we can see anything."

Boadie bounded ahead to the wall which stood about as high as her eyes. It was a wide wall built of rocks which had been roughly hewn, and fitted together without cement. It was easy to find a toehold, and Boadie stepped up and peered over the wall, with her elbows spread out on top of it on either side of her. She hung there for a moment, then dropped down.

"Nothing in sight," she said. "No people and no puppies. Let's walk on and take a look at the other side of the house."

They walked along, looking up at the red-tiled roof beyond the wall. When they had passed it, Boadie again hitched herself up and took a view of the territory. She turned around and smiled at Danny.

"He's here! Come, I'll give you a boost."

Quickly she jumped down, and then with some helpful shoves and heaves she managed to get Danny safely landed on top of the wall. Soon she had scrambled up beside him and while they were recovering their breath they took in the peaceful scene below them. The Bixton household seemed to be entirely deserted. A line of clothes blew peacefully back and forth in the sea breeze, but everything else was still. The only sign of life came from a small black and white puppy, lying full length on his stomach on a cool flagstone beside the kitchen door. His eyes blinked at them sleepily; then they closed again.

"Let's call to him," whispered Danny.

"Wait a minute or two," cautioned Boadie. "We must listen a while for sounds in the house. When we're sure it's safe, we can start to talk to him."

The two children might have been turned into two stones on top of the wall, they sat so still. The buzzing of cicadas in a large clump of pines below the house sounded loud to them; then, somewhere in the village below, came the sound of a man's voice, far away, calling, "Yaaa Yousef!"

A little lizard came out on the wall and went to sleep near Danny. The puppy opened his eyes to snap half-heartedly at a fly; then he dozed off again.

Finally Boadie said, "We're safe. Let's jump down into the yard and make friends with him."

Danny said a little fearfully, "But can we get out of there quickly if — if we need to?"

Boadie pointed along the wall a little way, where an old kitchen table stood. Some trays were resting on it, holding figs which had been spread out to dry in the sun.

"There's how we can climb back," she explained.

As softly as possible, the two thudded to the ground and found themselves inside the yard with the puppy. The pup had leaped up and run off when he heard them coming down, and now he was shrinking back into the corner formed by the kitchen steps, trembling and cowering.

"It's a beastly shame," said Boadie. "See how frightened he is? That shows you how he has been treated."

"Shall I pick him up and comfort him?" asked Danny.

"No, don't go near him," warned Boadie. "It would only frighten him. We must sit quietly here and talk to him until he learns we're his friends. Then he'll come to us himself."

They sat down cross-legged and began to talk to the little fellow.

"Good doggie, nice puppy," said Boadie.

"Good doggie, nice puppy," echoed Danny.

Boadie reached into the pocket of her dress and unrolled a small piece of Arab bread. In the center of it was a rather mashed-looking brown mass. "Piece of meatball I saved from lunch," she explained briefly.

Breaking off a little piece, she held it toward the puppy.

"Here, boy," she said softly. "I know he won't take it from my hand, but before I give it to him I want him to know it's from me."

The puppy lifted his nose slightly but he did not move.

"Here, little fellow, this is for you," murmured Boadie invitingly. Then, moving very slowly on her hands and knees, she reached out and set the piece on the kitchen step near the puppy, and returned to her former position.

Breathlessly the children watched the puppy take a step forward toward the meat. He lifted his nose and sniffed it once; then he pulled it down off the step and ate it. It was gone in a second; then he sat down where he was and regarded the donors.

"Now it's your turn, Danny," said Boadie, handing him a bit of meatball. "Do it the same way. Talk to him first, so he'll know it's you who's giving it; then lay it down near him and come back. Move slowly. You have to be very tactful. His feelings have been hurt too often."

Danny approached the puppy gently, murmuring in a very low tone of voice. He laid the meat down, and again the puppy ate it. This time after it was gone, he did not sit down, but stood watching them hopefully, tipping his head to one side.

"It's going to take us some time to teach him to be brave enough to run away," said Boadie. She added mournfully, "If only your brothers weren't so fussy we could just *take* him."

"We can't *steal* him," said Danny stoutly.

"Oh I know," said Boadie. "But we'll jolly well do everything we can to show him how to run away."

"All by himself," said Danny firmly.

"All by himself," Boadie reassured him. "But the minute he's out of this yard he'll have loving hands to help him."

She reached in her pocket again and pulled out a small wooden spool tied to a thread.

"Maybe he'll play a little now," she said.

Carefully she laid the spool near the puppy; then she returned to where Danny was sitting, holding the end of the thread. The puppy stepped up near the spool and sniffed it. Presently he put out a paw and touched it. Boadie gave the thread a little pull and the spool rolled a few inches. This startled the puppy. He looked at it for a moment; then crouched down on the ground and sprang onto the spool. Both the children laughed softly. As the puppy hung on to the spool, his sharp little teeth bit into it, and his tail moved. For a long time they sat there, Boadie gently twitching the thread, and the puppy fiercely attacking the spool.

At last Boadie handed the thread to Danny and stood up, remarking, "Here, you play with him a bit while I look around."

"Are you going anywhere?" asked Danny in sudden alarm.

"No — I'm right here. I'm just looking for a good running-away place. We can't expect the puppy to climb over that wall. — All by himself, that is," she added mischievously.

Presently, "I've found it!" she exclaimed.

"Found what?" asked Danny, absorbed in watching the puppy.

"The running-away place!" said Boadie. "Look here!"

On the far side of the yard, away from the house, was a place where a drainage pipe had evidently once led through the wall. A hole remained there; too small for a person to go through, but not too small for a puppy.

"See if he follows the spool over to this side of the yard," commanded Boadie.

Danny gently urged the puppy along, pulling the spool ahead of him. The puppy followed warily. Halfway across the yard he came. Then suddenly he lost all his courage and turning around he ran back and cowered against the kitchen wall.

"He heard something!" said Boadie. "Listen!"

The two children stood still. A front door banged, and Edmund's voice sounded loud and impatient.

"Mother! Where's everybody?"

"Quick, Danny!" ordered Boadie. "Up on the table!"

She boosted him on to the table; then as he climbed up from there to the wall she ran back to the puppy.

"Here, little fellow," she whispered, rapidly dumping down the remains of the meatball on the ground beside him. "We'll be back!"

She flew to the table and climbed up on the wall beside Danny. The kitchen door was starting to open.

"Hurry!" she said, jumping and pulling Danny wildly down on top of her.

They landed in a dusty heap in the road, right under the startled nose of a donkey, who stopped short. An old man on the back of the donkey regarded them in amazement as they picked themselves up and stepped to one side.

"In the name of the Cross!" he exclaimed piously in Arabic.

Then as Danny politely greeted him, "Marhaba!" he replied automatically, "Marhabtain!" A smile spread over his leathery brown face, and he nodded and murmured "Amerkan!" as if that explained everything. Then as the donkey plodded forward through the dust, the old man closed his eyes and went to sleep again, nodding and smiling.

Boadie and Danny followed along behind him.

"Well, we've made a start today anyway," said Boadie. "All we need now is the right time and opportunity." She chuckled a little to herself. "Edmund sounded as if he were in a bad humor! I wonder how the boys got along at the trenches."

The boys had been climbing the mountain in silence. There was no real path on this side of the mountain, north of the ruined house and around the shoulder of the slope. Hundreds of tiny paths made by the feet of goats led between bushes and brambles, leading into each other and in all directions. The boys called them goat paths. Once Danny had called them "ghost paths" and Harry was thinking it was a good name, for sometimes a little ghost path would lead you straight into a cliff; a place where a goat — or a ghost — could climb up with ease; but a boy could not — at least, not a boy who was full of tea and sand tarts at the moment. Harry was following Gerald and not paying much attention to where they were going, so he was surprised when he looked up and suddenly saw the trenches were just above them. A short steep scramble brought them to the top, and the boys sat down on the edge to catch their breath.

The trench behind them was deep enough to hide a man of average height. In places the wall of it was built up with stones; in other places the trench was carved right into the rock. Behind the trench the mountain rose in a gentler slope as they were now nearer the top of it. On this slope above them small pines grew out of the stony ground.

"Seems a pity," murmured Harry. "All this work, and then these trenches were never used."

"It's a good thing they weren't," said Gerald emphatically. "But what a lookout!"

He gazed at Beirut on the plain far below them, and at the vast stretch of sea reaching to the horizon.

"Well, I don't see Edmund anywhere," said Harry practically.

"He couldn't creep up on us from below," replied Gerald. "But he could easily sneak along in the trench, or perhaps come down from above through the little pines."

Harry glanced nervously into the trench.

"This trench twists and winds around a lot. Don't you think we'd better walk along the edge of it a way and make sure he isn't in it?"

Gerald shrugged his shoulders.

"Why bother? The idea is to *let* him sneak up on us here and draw him away from the other place."

His voice had dropped almost to a whisper. The mountainside was very still, and the sound of a dog barking came clearly from the village below.

"I don't like it," whispered Harry. "I don't like sitting here waiting to be sneaked up on."

A sound from above them made them both turn sharply around. Stones were rattling noisily as if someone were hurrying down around the crest of the mountain.

"He isn't much of a stalker, is he?" said Gerald scornfully. "What a noise! Here he comes — now look as if we were interrupted doing something very interesting."

The footsteps suddenly stopped just above them, and the boys looked up to see the face of a goat peering around a

rock at them. They burst into a roar of laughter. The goat looked a little surprised; then the rest of him emerged from behind the rock and he began busily munching at a thorn bush near by.

Behind him came the sound of more and more footsteps and of little stones set rolling down the hill until it sounded like a small landslide approaching.

"Here comes the rest of the army!" remarked Gerald, and soon a whole regiment of goats had surrounded them, leaping over the trenches, climbing the rocks, stopping here and there to nibble at the tasty brambles. The herd seemed to be in no hurry to move on. They scattered around over the hillside below the trenches, looking for food, and now and then pushing one another away from some particularly juicy thorn bush.

"I wonder who's in charge of them," remarked Harry.

"Marhaba," came a voice above them in polite greeting, as if in answer to his question.

The boys looked around. On the other side of the trench a boy about their age was sitting, resting on his heels. He was dressed in the usual style of the Druse mountaineer; his tight striped shirt was tucked into the top of his wide, baggy trousers, and he wore a broad leather belt. Tilted forward on his head he wore a tan felt brimless cap in the shape of a cone. But what made the boys stare in surprise was that on top of this ordinary cap the boy seemed to be wearing an unusual sort of decoration.

"Marhabtain," said Gerald, suddenly remembering to return the greeting.

The boy's brown eyes twinkled with pleasure and he continued in Arabic, "You are Americans, but you speak Arabic well! Do you live near here?"

Gerald rose and waved in the direction of the village of Shemlan. This gesture had an odd effect on the boy's hat decoration. The little bundle of feathers hopped up and showed itself to be a small bird which now stood up in alarm as if poised for flight. The boy had evidently felt the

bird stir, for he put up both his hands and gently lifted his hat off and set it on his knee, talking to the bird soothingly. The bird settled down on the hat again, but it kept turning its head this way and that, inquiringly, watching the boys. The goatherd grinned up at them.

"Latifa is still a little afraid when other people are around. I found her last winter; one wing and one leg were broken, and I brought her home and took care of her."

"What do you feed her?" asked Harry, squatting down on his side of the trench for a closer look.

"I don't feed her anything now," replied the boy. "She is free and looks for her own food. There, Latifa — get along now and get something for yourself!"

Setting the hat on the ground, he gave her a gentle shove with his brown finger. The little bird hopped off among the bushes and began pecking around at invisible insects.

"Will she come back when you want her?" inquired Gerald.

"She comes when I whistle to her," replied the boy.

"Where do you live?" asked Gerald. "And what's your name?"

"My name is Braheem," replied the boy. "I live in Beisur — back over the mountain and overlooking the Damur River valley."

"We have been there," observed Gerald. "It's a good long walk from here."

"Not too far," replied Braheem. "But I should be starting off. Come on, you Latifa!"

The little bird was out of sight. Braheem stood up, set his cap back on his head, and putting his hand to his waist, he pulled out a reed pipe which was stuck in his belt. He smiled at Gerald and Harry.

"Now watch this. Latifa likes music. Someday she is going to sing for me."

Raising the pipe to his lips he played a few shrill notes. The little bird suddenly appeared from nowhere and settled down on his cap again, twisting its head and listening to the music. Braheem stopped suddenly. The bird chirped a few notes, then stopped.

"She is a bulbul," explained Braheem. "But it seems she has forgotten how to sing. Someday she will answer me with her own music."

The boys had watched, fascinated, and now Harry begged, "Please play for us once more before you go."

Braheem looked very pleased and squatted down again. He set his head a little to one side, and Latifa hopped over a bit on the cap to accommodate herself to the angle. Then Braheem closed his eyes and put the pipes to his lips again and played. The music was loud and shrill, and varied between only a few notes, but to the boys out there watching the sun getting low over the sea and feeling the breeze blowing up from below, it seemed well suited to the mountains and the airy spaces around them. At last Braheem stopped and stood up, wiping his mouth on the back of his hand, and tucked the pipes back into his belt.

At this moment an interruption caused the three boys to turn suddenly around. From somewhere near them came a loud nasal yell, "Yanh! Ya-a-anh! Ya-a-a-nh!" It was obviously a rude mimicry of the sound of the pipes. Braheem looked startled, but Gerald and Harry glanced at each other with sudden understanding. Then Edmund's grinning face appeared over the top of the trench a few feet away, followed by the rest of him.

"Your American friend doesn't like the pipe music," said Braheem, turning away.

"He's not our friend," replied Gerald. "And we do like the music. I don't know what's the matter with him."

Edmund had stopped, a little disappointed that no one had spoken to him, and obviously feeling left out by the interchange of Arabic words.

At Gerald's last words Braheem turned around once more and looked earnestly at Edmund.

"Ya-a-a-nh!" said Edmund.

Braheem shook his head slowly, and then turning to Gerald he raised his forefinger and revolved it in a circle near his own head.

"Poor fellow!" he said, "Poor fellow!"

Though his words were in Arabic, his forefinger made the meaning clear. With a wave of farewell to the boys he started off up the hill, giving a shrill whistle to his goats to follow him.

In delight Gerald turned to Edmund. He translated Braheem's remark for Edmund's benefit, adding a few of his own, and repeated the gesture.

"Poor fellow! He needs to have his head examined, that's all! Edmund, dear, try not to make such awful noises. Does it hurt so much to have a brain like yours?"

"Oh shut up!"

Edmund threw a stone in their direction, and started off down the hill.

"Shall we follow him?" asked Harry.

"No, let him go," said Gerald. "We'll hope he's learned a lesson in politeness this afternoon. Let's walk along the trenches instead, till we're at the top of the hill behind our house, and then go home by the regular path."

It was a winding route, for the trenches were made in a zigzag line. Soon the boys were around the shoulder of the mountain and in sight of the ruined house not far below them, and of their own house beyond. Here they paused to watch the sun getting low over the sea.

"The tennis court looks like a postage stamp from here," remarked Harry.

Gerald glanced at it, then brought his gaze nearer, to the ruined house.

"The next thing we must do," he said thoughtfully, "is find some excuse to go and see Miss Mariam. Then we can ask her what she knows about the people who lived in this little house."

"Why don't we just go ahead and ask her?" asked Harry. "Why do we need an excuse?"

"Well, we could," said Gerald, "but she might wonder why we're so interested all of a sudden. It would be better just to ask her casually. — Come on, let's go!" he ended suddenly, and with a leap and a yell he started headlong down the mountainside, scattering stones as he went, slipping and sliding on loose earth, leaping over small rocks and bushes, and dodging around large ones, his arms spread wide as he jumped and slid. Harry followed, rushing surefooted but helter-skelter in mad descent after his brother.

In a few minutes they shot into the back door of the house, nearly knocking over John, who stood calmly looking at them, munching a sandwich.

"Yafta wash your hands," he remarked. "Supper's ready."

"Then what are you eating a sandwich for?" inquired Gerald.

"Because I'm hungry," he replied sensibly. "Pa's doing the yawning," he added, rather unexpectedly.

A loud squeaking and rattling of pulleys from the front of the house drew their attention, and the three boys went out to the balcony to watch their father pull up the huge awning which had sheltered the big living room from the afternoon sun. The sun was dipping down into the sea now, and while their father wound the rope and fastened it, the boys leaned lazily against the balcony railing to watch the sun disappear. Their mother's voice behind them caused them to turn.

"I'm glad you're back, boys! I wanted to tell you that tomorrow Pa and I have to go to Souk for the day. We'll take John along with us. Danny too, if he wants. How would you like to take a picnic lunch on the mountain, and invite your friend Dorothy?"

"Good!" said Gerald. "But Danny can stay with us if he likes. Could we invite Miss Dunbar too?"

Their mother, in surprise, glanced over at their father. "You see, Boadie's supposed to have her along too," explained Gerald.

"And anyway we like her," added Harry.

"Of course you can invite her," replied their mother. "Dorothy — or Boadie — will be coming in any minute now with Danny, so we can give her the invitation. Supper's almost ready, so you'd better — "

" — wash our hands," said Gerald. "John told us."

"There's just one thing," added their mother as the boys were moving into the house. "Before you start on your picnic tomorrow I want you to run down to Miss Mariam's. I promised her an article in a magazine."

Gerald and Harry glanced at each other and smiled.

"Sure we will," said Gerald. "We'll be glad to."

"Miss Dunbar says we're a good influence on Boadie," observed Gerald complacently. He finished peeling a fresh fig and laid the peel out neatly on his plate.

"Ha — ha," remarked Boadie automatically, without rancor. She had finished her own breakfast earlier, and had arrived in time to watch the boys finishing theirs.

"A good influence," repeated Gerald, addressing himself to his parents and ignoring Boadie. "After we invited Boadie to the picnic today we happened to mention that we had this errand to do at Miss Mariam's, and Boadie wanted to come along. So she asked Miss Dunbar if she could have her lesson last night so she could be free this morning. I guess Miss Dunbar nearly fainted."

He was starting to peel another fig, and Boadie watched him fascinated. First he would slice a thin piece off the top of the fig, like a scalp, and set it with care on the edge of his plate. Then starting at the stem end he would peel off the rest of the skin in little strips. Boadie looked over at Harry's dish. He too had a border of little fig scalps lined up along the edge of his plate. Boadie counted them.

"My word! How many figs do you boys eat for breakfast?"

"We can have as many figs as we are old," explained Harry.

Boadie frowned. She was not one to tell on a friend, but she had counted the scalps and she was pretty sure that

Gerald was not fifteen years old. Gerald saw her expression and explained.

"Don't forget what Pa said when we asked him how soon we could eat all the figs we wanted."

"I remember," murmured Harry. He was busy counting Gerald's scalps.

"I don't," said his father. "What did I say?"

Gerald looked at him reproachfully. "You said that when we were old enough to go to the Arabic service on Sundays we'd be old enough to eat all the figs we want."

Pa cleared his throat. "Well, if I said that I stand by it."

Gerald reached happily for another fig. His mother interposed: "Oh Harry, do you really think — ?"

"Hold on a moment, Gerald," continued his father. "Just how long have you been attending Arabic service?"

"I began last Sunday," Gerald stated. "Now I am going regularly."

"It seems to me that that remains to be seen," observed his father. "Suppose you ease up on those figs now. This week you might have one fig beyond your age limit; next week two, and so on. Then by next year if you find that this Arabic service has been established as a habit, you will have reached an age where — presumably — you have enough sense to know when to stop on the figs."

"Well, it's all very confusing to me," Boadie observed later as they were starting down the road toward Miss Mariam's. "I don't see what figs have got to do with Arabic services."

"It's all a matter of age," explained Gerald grandly. "You've got to be fairly grown-up to sit patiently through a service which you don't understand."

"But you do understand Arabic," objected Boadie. "I've heard you and Harry talking it lots of times."

"Not church Arabic," said Gerald. "They use book Arabic in church. And written-down Arabic is different from spoken Arabic."

"Like Shakespeare, or the Bible?" suggested Boadie.

"Harder than that," interposed Harry. "There are different words for the same thing. Like 'cat.' In spoken Arabic it's 'bsayni.' But in written Arabic it's 'hurr.' "

"There!" exclaimed Boadie. "See, you do know some written Arabic after all, and you just said you didn't."

"That word is in the Arabic primer I'm studying," said Harry. Then he added gloomily, "But they don't talk about cats much in church."

Danny had been walking along listening eagerly to the conversation, listening so eagerly in fact that he kept getting in Harry's way.

"Look, Danny," finally expostulated Harry. "Would you mind walking a little faster or else not walking *just* in front of me? I keep stepping on your heels."

Danny obligingly moved to one side.

"When *I* say 'cat' in Arabic I say 'beesy,' " he remarked.

His brothers chuckled. "That means 'pussy' in Arabic," they explained to Boadie. "That's when you're really fond of a cat."

"Well, I like all cats," maintained Danny stoutly. "And dogs too. Puppies especially."

Boadie gave him a wink. Danny gave a little hop of delight which nearly landed him on Harry's foot again.

By now they were nearing the steps which led down to Miss Mariam's cottage.

"Isn't it awfully early to go visiting?" asked Boadie in sudden shyness. "The sun's hardly on our side of the mountains yet."

"It's not too early for Shemlan," replied Gerald.

"Nobody sleeps late in Shemlan," said Harry, "except a few dopey Westerners. The mountain people get up early and do their work while it's cool. Then in the middle of the day when it's hot, they take a rest."

"I can see Miss Mariam now," said Danny. "She's just letting the cat in at the back door. Miss Mariam!" he called, and started running down the stone steps.

Miss Mariam stepped out of the back door and waved to them, then, smiling, she started up the stone steps to meet Danny. Soon they were all shaking hands, and Boadie was introduced.

"Come right down to the living room," said Miss Mariam. "You boys have been so busy I've hardly seen you lately, and this is the first time that Dorothy has been here." As she reached the front door of her little house, under the shade of the big oak tree, she paused a moment and untied the apron she had on, folding it and laying it on a stool in the doorway.

Just as if we were grown-up visitors, thought Boadie approvingly.

Then to Boadie's surprise, instead of inviting them into the house, she led the way right past the front door. Two more wide stone steps brought them down into a flat, closed-in terrace, which gave the effect of an outdoor room with the oak tree for a roof. On one side a rough stone wall separated the terrace from the field beyond; the other two sides of the square were enclosed by two wide stone settees. Long quilted pads were laid along the seats to soften them, and thick stiff pillows were set against the stone backs. The floor of the area was hard-packed earth, swept clean, and a little table stood in the middle, with some books on it.

Over it all spread the great green branches of the old tree, whispering and rustling in the morning breeze, and casting a cool deep shade over the outdoor living room.

"What a lovely lovely room!" exclaimed Boadie as she sat down on the stone seat. "Do you live out here all the time?"

"Most of the time," said Miss Mariam smiling. "In the summer, that is. You know it doesn't rain in Shemlan from May till September."

She excused herself and went off into the house, where the children could hear the pleasant sound of glasses being set out on a tray. Soon she was back with lemonade and a little dish of sugared almonds which she passed around. Gerald remembered the errand on which they had come, and laid his mother's magazine on the table.

"Ma says not to bother to return it. She has finished reading it."

"Thank you," said Miss Mariam. "And would you mind taking her this little recipe? I promised to write it out for her."

She handed Gerald a piece of paper which he carefully put in the pocket of his shirt.

"Can I see your cat?" asked Danny, who had quickly finished his lemonade.

"Yes, we'll call him," replied Miss Mariam. She added a little sadly, "He stays in the house a lot more nowadays. He's afraid of the boy next door who throws stones at him."

"I'll go find him," said Danny.

As he went off into the house, Harry nudged Gerald. Gerald scowled at him. Then he remarked in a strictly casual fashion, "We are going on a picnic today."

"Well, you'll have a good time, I know," said Miss Mariam. "Where are you planning to go?"

"Oh, up on the hill behind our house. Near that little ruined house." Gerald stopped being casual, and plunged ahead. "Do you know anything about that little house, Miss Mariam? Who lived there, and why they lived so far from the village, and why the house is ruined now?"

"So many questions!" smiled Miss Mariam. Then she replied slowly, "It has been many years since I have thought about that little house. Yes, I can tell you what I know about it."

She folded her hands on her lap, and into her eyes came a faraway, dreamy look as if she was remembering things that had happened long ago.

"When I was a little girl, my brother and I used to play all over the mountainside, just the way you do today. But I remember that somehow we never liked to play near that little house, although it wasn't ruined then. An old lady lived there, named Im Butrus. That means 'Mother of Butrus, or Peter,'" explained Miss Mariam turning to Boadie. "She wasn't friendly to us children. At least she didn't like us to play near her house and she would shoo us away." Miss Mariam sighed. "I suppose we children used to go near her house on purpose sometimes just to tease her, at first. Then somehow we stopped going near her house because we were afraid. The story got around that she could put the 'evil eye' on us, as we say in Arabic. That is, that she could use magic to harm us. In other words, you might say that we began to think of her as a sort of witch."

Miss Mariam stopped and sighed again. "Poor woman. Of course it was all nonsense — about her being a witch, I mean. It wasn't till much later that I heard her story. Once she had lived here in the village with her husband and her only son. Her husband died when the boy was still young, but the boy Butrus grew up to be a fine young fellow. He worked hard and took good care of his mother, and even found time to study. After he had finished the village school he borrowed books from the schoolmaster in the next town. Yet he must have been good fun, too. The other young men liked him, and they still tell stories in the village about some of the jokes he played on his friends. Yes, Butrus must have been quite a boy." She smiled and paused before going on.

"Yet he got into trouble too. He was argumentative. From his books he had gotten some ideas which the other villagers didn't agree with. Once some police even came to Shemlan to investigate him. It seemed that someone had overheard him saying something against the government. The sheikh of the village had a hard time persuading them that Butrus didn't mean anything by it." She chuckled a little. "It seemed that Butrus wouldn't help. He refused to say that he didn't mean what he had said. He was an obstinate young man."

"Good for him!" said Gerald.

Miss Mariam continued speculatively, "Of course nobody here in the village really liked the government; it was no fun being ruled by outsiders. But most of the villagers knew it was wiser to keep their mouths shut, and they didn't like to have Butrus cause trouble.

"Well, one summer Butrus started building a little house up on the mountain. The neighbors all asked him why he was moving up there, but he never could give them a satisfactory answer. He'd say that the climate was better up there, or that he liked the view, or that there was more room to move around, or all sorts of silly answers till his friends got annoyed and said well if he wanted to be so exclusive, let him.

"Then came the day when the house was finished, and Butrus started moving all their furniture up the mountain, on donkey-back. I remember my mother telling me about it long afterwards. She went to see Im Butrus and found her in tears. My mother talked severely to Butrus. She said to him, 'It's all very well for you to go and live up there by yourself, but why do you have to drag your mother up there — away from the village, away from her friends, away from the house where she has lived all these years?' "

"She was right," said Boadie. "What did Butrus say to that?"

"That's what was so odd," said Miss Mariam. "He didn't answer my mother at all. He walked over to his own mother, put his hands gently on her two shoulders, and looking into her eyes he said to her, 'Mother, you hear what our neighbor and friend has just said to me. Isn't she right? Isn't it better for you to stay down here?' And then, even with the tears rolling down her cheeks, his mother shook her head, and replied that she was determined to go with him. My mother was very indignant, but there was nothing more that she could say. She said she had a strange feeling, at that point, as though the mother and son were discussing things which she knew nothing about."

"So they lived there together," said Gerald. "Did you ever see Butrus?"

"I may have but I don't remember him," said Miss Mariam. "For a year they lived there together, and then one day Butrus told people in the village that he had to go to Beirut for a week or two on business. My mother invited

Im Butrus to come and stay at our house while her son was away, but the old lady said no, she preferred to sleep at home. They had a big dog anyway, and she was not afraid. So Butrus went off to Beirut." Miss Mariam paused. Then she concluded: "And no one ever saw Butrus again."

Boadie gave a long, shivering sigh. "What do you think happened to him?"

"Nobody ever found out," said Miss Mariam. "People made inquiries in Beirut, and there were rumors that he had been seen there, but no real clues could be found. My father believed that the foreign government finally got hold of him. Anyhow, he never came back.

"His mother continued to live in the little house. She never gave up hope that her son would come back. After a year or two her relatives came over from Souk and tried to persuade her to come and live with them. But she would not be persuaded; she simply kept repeating, 'When he comes back, he will find me waiting for him.' She kept his bedroll in the corner of the house, with a fresh cover always sewed on it, and always she had two dishes, two cups, two of everything ready in case he should come.

"By the time I was old enough to be running around the mountainside with my brother, Im Butrus had withdrawn a good deal from the village people. She would go down once a week or so to get things she needed. She made lace that she would sell, but I think she had enough money to live on from the rent of the little house in the village. At first the other village women used to go up to visit her, but she didn't seem very welcoming. And finally they gave it up. It was a long hot walk up the mountain when you weren't sure of a welcome at the end of the walk. Perhaps she realized that the village women were beginning to think she was a little crazy."

There was a small silence.

"It's strange how differently you see things as you grow older," said Miss Mariam sadly. "It must have been a terribly lonely life for her up there alone, always hoping for someone who never came. And yet, you know, when she died some four or five years later, they said she had a very peaceful look on her face."

"Did she die alone there?" asked Boadie.

Miss Mariam nodded. "She seemed to have died very peacefully in her sleep — probably a heart attack. Her relatives came and put the house in order and packed the things away. Nobody, it seemed, wanted to live in the little house any more, so it has been left to fall into ruins."

Miss Mariam stood up. "Now that's enough of a sad little story. Let's see if Danny has been having a good visit with the cat."

"I'm bringing him out," said Danny, coming out of the door.

The large white cat was almost too large an armful for him, and he seemed to be in danger of spilling it on the floor. He hesitated, then squatted down and set the cat on the step. Boadie jumped up and walked toward him.

"Beesy, beesy!" she called coaxingly. The cat came to her and rubbed against her brown legs.

Miss Mariam laughed.

"You seem to know Arabic cat-language," she remarked.

"Oh I've been learning Arabic from Danny," explained Boadie airily.

"Miss Mariam, we must be going," said Gerald standing up. "We have to get started on our picnic."

"Well, come again soon," urged Miss Mariam.

She opened a drawer in the table and took out a large piece of white letter paper. Laying it on the table she emptied the rest of the sugared almonds into the paper and twisted the corners up to form a little package. She handed this to Gerald.

"For the picnic," she said. "Have a happy time!"

Gerald thanked her. As he pushed the package into his trousers pocket, he remarked to Miss Mariam, "It's too bad that young man couldn't be here to see his country now that it is free."

"I was thinking of that too," said Miss Mariam softly. "We don't have our independence yet, but the French have promised it to us someday."

After the children had left, she walked up two or three of the steps toward the road, until the ruined house on the hill came into her view. For a few minutes she stood there, leaning against the stone wall, gazing up at the mountain. Then with a little sigh she turned back to the house and picking up her apron, slowly tied it on again.

I THOUGHT MAYBE I wouldn't like this little house any more," remarked Boadie. "You know — after Miss Mariam's story about the evil eye and so on. But it seems the same as ever — not scary at all. Just a little sad perhaps." She was sitting on a rock near the edge of the terrace, staring at the ruined house in front of her. She had set a teakettle on the ground beside her, and in her lap was a basket she had been carrying up the hill in her other hand.

No answer came from Gerald and Harry. They were using their breath to get up the last steep bit of the path, and between them they carried a long roll of matting. Gerald had a knapsack on his back, and each of the boys had a canteen slung over one shoulder. Behind them, following along more slowly, came Miss Dunbar with Danny behind her. Miss Dunbar was carrying an old broom over her shoulder, and the pockets of her wide trousers bulged in a most unusual way. Over one arm she carried a folding campstool. Danny wore his knapsack and was carrying a stout wooden board which was as high as his shoulder. It was an awkward thing to carry, and Gerald had offered to carry it for him, but Danny wanted to bring it himself.

"It's for the little house," he said. "I found it myself down near the bottom of the driveway."

"What are you going to use it for?" asked Gerald.

"I haven't decided yet," replied Danny. "It could be put across two stones, to use for a bench or a table, or it could be a shelf for collections — or anything." So he had brought it along. He had no canteen but he carried his own drinking water, for a vinegar bottle with a cork in the top protruded from his knapsack. Miss Dunbar and Boadie had maintained that they wanted no cold water; that tea was what they wanted on a picnic.

In a few minutes the whole party had reached the terrace.

"Let's start fixing up the house right away!" suggested Boadie impatiently.

"First we must put all the picnic things in a safe place out of the sun," said Gerald. "Especially the water. Danny's cave would be a cool safe spot."

While the boys piled their luggage into the cave, Miss Dunbar leaned the broom against the wall of the house and unfolded her campstool. Danny, who had just left his knapsack in the cave, came back as she was setting up the stool. He had found that studying Miss Dunbar was almost as interesting as studying the ants.

"Are you going to paint this morning — or are you just going to think?" he inquired.

Miss Dunbar smiled. "Neither," she replied. "This morning I am going to sit here on this campstool and make suggestions. Nobody needs to follow them however, as school is out today. And the first suggestion I would make," she continued, raising her voice a little as Gerald crawled out from the cave, "is that somebody might build a fireplace and start the kettle heating."

"Come on, Danny," said Gerald; "I'll show you how to build one. We must decide where to build it, so that the smoke won't blow on us where we want to sit."

He wet his finger in his mouth and held it up. Danny did the same thing, somewhat mystified but always willing.

"The side of your finger that feels cold is the side toward the wind," explained Gerald. "We'll put the fireplace over here, just beyond the entrance to the cave. We'll need three good-sized rocks to make the back and the sides of the fireplace; but they must be flat on top so we can rest the kettle on them."

Boadie and Harry had joined them now and everybody set to work looking for the best rocks.

"Here's a beauty to start with!" announced Miss Dunbar. The children looked up in surprise. Miss Dunbar had evidently forgotten that she was only giving suggestions, and having abandoned her campstool was now clinging precariously to the face of the cliff.

"Look out!" she warned, and sent a large rock crashing down. With a leap she followed the rock, landing on her feet and brushing off the front of her trousers.

"A bit of a job, that, but it's just the right shape for the back of the fireplace, and I couldn't resist going after it."

"Good," said Gerald with approval. He set it up in place, just as Harry and Boadie arrived with two others.

"Now we need fuel," announced Gerald. "The best thing to make a good hot fire quickly is some bilan."

"I wish you'd talk English," complained Boadie. "What's bilan?"

"This stuff," said Gerald, kicking a low tightly grown bush of brambles by his feet. "Makes a wonderful fire — hot and even. They use it in the village ovens."

"Come to think of it, I've seen the donkeys going by loaded with it," said Boadie. "But I'm not volunteering to pick it for you."

"It's not hard," said Gerald. "But you don't pick it. Look."

Putting his toe under one side of the round little bush he pushed it to one side and stepped on it, exposing the short woody stem that anchored it to the ground. Then pulling out his pocketknife he cut the stem. The whole bush came free and he gave it a kick, rolling it in the direction of the fireplace.

"I'll cut the bilan if the rest of you will go on up above the cliff and collect a few sticks from under the pine trees."

It did not take Harry and Boadie and Danny very long to collect an armful of sticks and dry pine branches. When they returned, Gerald had finished setting the rocks into a good solid fireplace, and Miss Dunbar was vigorously sweeping small stones and other debris out of the house. In no time, a bright fire was blazing and crackling away under the kettle.

"Come on, Harry, let's spread the matting down and fix up the house for the picnic! It'll be like Miss Mariam's outdoor living room," Boadie explained.

Harry pulled the roll of matting over to the doorway, and together they spread the matting over the earthen floor. When it was done, they stood back and looked at the effect. The little house now suddenly looked very settled and domestic. Danny, peering in through the low, large window, immediately climbed in over the sill and sat down cross-legged in the middle of the matting.

"What a difference it makes!" exclaimed Harry.

"It's beautiful!" said Boadie. Their exclamations brought Miss Dunbar and Gerald to the door.

"Let's roll in some big stones for seats," suggested Gerald.

"But I'm getting so hungry!" pleaded Danny. "And besides, this mat is so comfortable to sit on."

"Didn't I hear somebody suggesting a picnic table of some sort?" queried Miss Dunbar vaguely.

"My board!" exclaimed Danny.

"Come on, Harry; help me roll in two stones to set Danny's board on." In a minute Gerald and Harry had found two of fairly equal height, and the board placed across them made a rather narrow but adequate table. Danny brought Miss Dunbar's campstool in and set it at the head, and Boadie brought in the picnic basket and the knapsacks. She and Miss Dunbar began arranging the food on the table.

"My blessed aunt!" murmured Boadie happily. "Your mother put in enough food here to feed the whole village. Look at these lovely little pies!"

Gerald glanced over and his eyes gleamed with anticipation.

"Those are samboosics!" he said. "Little Arab pies with meat and pine nuts inside. Maybe you'd better not try them, Boadie, if you're not used to Arab food," he said with sudden solicitude.

"Don't be a pig," replied Boadie severely. "There are plenty for you and me both." She was peering into a large bowl tied up in a white napkin. "Is this something Arab too?" she asked.

"No, that's American potato salad. I hope we brought a spoon with us somewhere," replied Gerald.

"I have the forks and spoons in my knapsack," said Danny.

"Here's your knapsack; I'll get them out," Gerald offered, unpacking a roll of cutlery and setting it on the table. "But didn't I tell you to bring a bottle of water too?" he asked. "It isn't in here."

Danny smiled. "It's keeping cool. Come and see!"

Gerald reluctantly rose from his knees. "Well, I guess you'd better have it if we're going to eat lunch now." He followed Danny into the cave.

"I buried it!" said Danny. "See, feel how cool and soft this earth is. I thought it would keep the bottle cool."

The neck of the bottle was sticking up out of the floor of the cave, and Gerald watched Danny dig out the soft black earth from around it. A new idea was beginning to stir around in his head.

"Danny, you know what we forgot to do?"

"No, what?" asked Danny helpfully.

"What dopes!" Gerald was looking thoughtfully around the cave. "We thought we had examined this cave so carefully. But we forgot the very simplest thing. We must excavate!" Then, seeing Danny's bewildered face, "Dig, I mean!"

Boadie's voice was calling them impatiently. "Come along, you two! The kettle's boiling and everything's ready!"

"We'll tell the others at lunch," said Gerald. "Maybe we can start work this afternoon."

Half an hour later the group was sitting or lying stretched out on the matting in various attitudes of satisfaction and fullness.

"There's a whole shoe box full of grapes and plums that nobody has touched yet," said Harry.

"Save it for tea time," said Gerald. "We'll have our picnic stretch over the whole day." He was sitting on the ground, his back against the wall of the house, in the shade. "If you people stuff yourselves any more you won't be able to help me dig in the cave."

"You ate five samboosics yourself," Harry pointed out.

"A man who does heavy labor needs food," replied Gerald with dignity. "Now what about tools for digging?" he asked, changing the subject.

"There's the potato salad spoon," suggested Harry.

"No you don't!" interposed Boadie firmly. "Your mother isn't here to protect her property, but I will. No digging with the old family silver. You boys are just plain lazy," she went on severely. "The only thing to do, and you know it, is to go down to the house and get the things we need for digging. — I'll go down and help you," she ended kindly.

Gerald looked at Harry and groaned. "She's right. But I don't feel like it."

Miss Dunbar, who had assumed her thinking position stretched out on one end of the mat, now spoke from under the hat which covered her face.

"If I might suggest — "

There was a short silence, so Gerald spoke to the hat.

"Yes, Miss Dunbar?"

"This is no moment for great activity. The Greeks always used to relax after a feast." There was silence again, and Gerald thought she had dropped off to sleep. But the voice came out softly again, a little muffled from under the hat. "'So after they had stayed desire for drink and food, then in their thoughts they turned to other things, the song and dance; for these attend a feast.'"

"Pardon?" said Boadie.

"A quotation from the *Odyssey*," murmured Miss Dunbar.

"Is that the book that you have in your pocket?" asked Harry.

"Yes, as a matter of fact, it is," affirmed the voice.

"Is it an interesting story?" asked Danny.

"Very," replied Miss Dunbar. Suddenly the hat came off her face, and with a swift sort of whirling motion she sat up, her legs crossed like an Arab. She fished the book out of her pocket and slapped it onto the ground in front of her. She fixed her gaze on Danny, and Gerald, looking at her black-fringed eyes of clear gray, wondered again how old — or how young — she was.

"That book, Danny, is one of the oldest stories in the world, and the most romantic."

"I don't care for love stories," said Danny politely.

Miss Dunbar laughed. "This is an adventure story — it starts with a woman and ends with one, but mostly it's about a man."

"What did he do?" asked Danny.

"He went off to war when he was a young man and people at home thought he had disappeared forever. Only one woman believed that he was still alive, and that he would come back some day. That was his wife Penelope."

"Why — that was like that poor old woman Im Butrus," said Boadie, " — the one who lived right here!"

Miss Dunbar nodded, and for a moment the little group was silent. A cicada started shrilling loudly above them, and the sea breeze whispered through the dry thistles outside the little house's windows.

"I don't care for sad stories, either," said Danny in a small voice.

"But this one has a happy ending," Miss Dunbar reassured him. "You see he did come back in the end. Penelope was still waiting for him, twenty years after he left to go to war."

"What was the war about?" asked Gerald who always liked to get the facts.

"About Helen, the queen of a neighboring country. Helen was stolen away from her husband, and our hero went to help her husband bring her back. She was the most beautiful woman in the world."

"What did she look like?" demanded Gerald, again after the facts.

"She was 'long-robed,' and 'white-armed,' and 'royal,' and a 'queen of women,' " replied Miss Dunbar.

"Did she have red hair?" asked Danny.

Miss Dunbar smiled a little and glanced at Boadie, who looked pleased at the unconscious compliment.

"Perhaps," said Miss Dunbar.

"What did you say the man's name was?" asked Danny. "The one who was gone so long?"

"Odysseus. Or some people call him Ulysses. And now to go back to my original suggestion — the song and dance. Is anyone here musical?"

No one volunteered. Presently Gerald picked up Danny's empty vinegar bottle, and blowing into it produced one low prolonged bass note.

"It sounds like a ghost moaning," said Boadie with delight. "Here, do let me try it!" The bottle was passed around and everyone had a blow. Harry blew the deep loud note resonantly, but Boadie and Danny laughed too much to produce any results.

"Won't you try it, Miss Dunbar?" invited Gerald passing her the bottle.

Miss Dunbar started to reach her hand out to take it, but she stopped midway.

"What in the world is that?" she exclaimed.

A sort of rumbling and rattling sound seemed to be getting nearer.

"It's the goats!" announced Gerald jumping up. "Better

get the leftover picnic things into the cave, or they'll be all over us!"

"For a moment I thought it was Boadie's landslide," said Harry as everyone began picking up the leftovers and putting them rapidly into baskets and knapsacks. It was not too soon, for already a whiskery face was peering inquisitively down at them over the ledge above. He was joined by another whiskery face with sad eyes. Soon all the picnic things were well stowed away in the cave. Miss Dunbar firmly set her campstool against the bush which covered the entrance, and sat down on it.

"There are plenty of other bushes for them to eat," she said, "and they shan't have this one."

"Marhaba," said a polite voice above them.

"Marhabtain, ya Braheem!" replied Gerald turning around.

A slow smile spread over Braheem's tanned face, as he squatted down on the ledge above them. As he settled down, Latifa flew off his hat and lit on the ledge near him, looking at the people below with her head cocked first on this side, then on that. Gerald couldn't help laughing. Miss Dunbar had stood up to see who the visitor was (keeping a firm foot on her campstool) and Boadie was staring entranced at the little bird.

"Is this the bird you told me about?" she asked.

"Yes," said Gerald. "That is Latifa, and that is Braheem." Then in Arabic he continued, addressing Braheem, "This lady is Miss Dunbar. And this is Boadie. And this is my brother Danny."

Smiles and bows were interchanged between the two English women and the Arab boy. To Danny Braheem said, "Do you speak Arabic?"

"Yes," replied Danny. "How are you?"

"Good boy!" said Braheem. "Look," he continued. "Latifa likes you."

Latifa, having looked the company over, had seemed to decide that the smallest one was for her. She had flown down off the ledge and was hopping cautiously toward Danny's foot. He stood very still. She came up all the way and gave his foot a quick peck; then she flew back up on the ledge.

Braheem laughed. "She'll be back to see you again," he said.

"Look," said Boadie; "isn't that his reed pipe sticking in his belt? Maybe now we can have some real music after our feast!"

Her eager gestures and questioning tone roused Braheem's curiosity. He looked at Gerald and waited for a translation.

"She wants you to play your pipes for her," Gerald explained.

Braheem made a little gesture of apology, but the smile on his face showed that he was pleased, and he pulled the pipe out, setting it to his lips.

"Just a minute!" interrupted Miss Dunbar. "Ask him what's wrong with his thumb."

Again Braheem hesitated, turning to Gerald for a translation. On the thumb of his right hand, which was holding the pipe, was a large unwieldy bandage.

"The lady is asking what happened to your thumb."

Braheem shrugged his shoulders and gave a brief reply. Gerald turned to Miss Dunbar.

"He says it's nothing. He cut it this morning and tied it up himself."

"Well it's a very dirty rag and I must see that thumb at

once. Harry, please come over here and keep our hairy
friends away from this stool." She gave a little push to a
goat who had come too near; he looked surprised and leaped
away down the hill. Then Miss Dunbar took a step toward
the ledge and spoke directly to Braheem in English.

"Now, young man, please come right down; you can
scramble down between those rocks over there. I want to
have a look at your thumb." Her pointing finger showed
him how he was to come.

"Yes ma'am," he said politely in Arabic, and came on
down to see what this interesting lady wanted of him.

As soon as he was before her, Miss Dunbar took his hand
firmly and began untying the bandage.

"You must excuse me — this bandage is very dirty," said
Braheem, in Arabic.

In English Miss Dunbar remarked, "A horrible old bandage. Imagine putting a dirty thing like that on a wound."

"I'm very sorry," continued Braheem; "going around with the goats all day I can't keep it clean. I'm embarrassed to have the lady touch it."

The bandage was off now, and Miss Dunbar walked over to the fireplace and dropped it on the coals which were still red.

"But it's the only piece of rag I have with me!" expostulated Braheem (in Arabic).

"Now just stop worrying," said Miss Dunbar (in English). "Sit right down here on this campstool. Just move away please, Harry. The goats won't come as long as he's on it. Gerald, please bring the kettle here. The boiled water is still warm, and we can wash his finger with it."

While she was talking she had pulled out of her pocket a large clean handkerchief which she unfolded and spread on the ground. Next she produced the small tin candy box labeled "First Aid," and laid it on the handkerchief, taking out of it a small roll of cotton, a narrow gauze bandage, and a little bottle of iodine, which she set out beside the box. Fishing in her pocket again, she drew out a large pair of scissors. When these were added to the display on the handkerchief, Braheem murmured a pious Arabic exclamation of dismay. Miss Dunbar seemed to understand because she pointed to the scissors and then to the gauze and assured him (in English) that there was nothing to fear.

"Now just hold your thumb out over here and we'll pour some clean water on it," she said, and Braheem obediently held his thumb under the trickle of water.

"Then we'll clean it a little more thoroughly." Miss Dunbar picked up a generous wad of cotton and poured a little water on it; then she gently dabbed the cut until it was clean. A second wad of cotton was dampened with the iodine and as she laid it on the wound she said, "Steady now — this will hurt." As he winced from the pain she patted him on the shoulder.

"Now you're going to be all right." In a minute the gauze bandage was securely in place and Miss Dunbar was repacking the first aid things into the box.

"Thank you, ma'am," said Braheem faintly (in Arabic).

Miss Dunbar eyed him kindly. "Now it just so happens that I was saving a little treat for us all for tea. But I think this is the time to bring it out so you can have some too."

She walked over to a wide crack between two of the stones high in the house wall, and drew out a package.

"I thought it might melt if I kept it in my pocket," she explained. Unwrapping it she disclosed two large bars of chocolate which she divided up among the entire party, with the largest piece going to Braheem. As she handed it to him he thanked her and rose from his seat.

"I feel all right now," he explained. "Let the lady sit down." Miss Dunbar accepted the seat, and the four children sat on the ground near by. Braheem ate part of his piece and carefully wrapped the rest up for later.

"What did you say the lady's name was?" he asked Gerald.

"Miss Dunbar," said Gerald.

"Miss Dumba," repeated Braheem looking up at her respectfully. Miss Dunbar smiled at him.

"And now what about some of that music?" she asked pointing to his pipes.

Braheem smiled and touched his finger to his forehead.

Then raising the pipes he began to play. As the loud, skirling music rose, Latifa suddenly appeared on the piper's hat and sat still, giving her full attention to it. When the music stopped, Boadie heaved a sigh.

"That's jolly good. Tell him I liked it, will you?" she said to Gerald.

Gerald translated her remark, as closely as he could, into Arabic. It took him several sentences while Boadie waited wonderingly.

"Did I say all *that?*" she demanded in amazement.

Braheem smiled and touched his hand to his forehead.

"Well — you see I had to say it in the Arab way," explained Gerald.

"Just what did you say I said?"

"Oh, something like this: 'May God bless your lips, and may the name of God be upon you; the music was sweet as the song of a nightingale on a moonlight night.' "

Boadie was silent with awe at her own eloquence. Miss Dunbar remarked dryly, "A bit loud for a nightingale. I should say more like the Scottish bagpipes skirling away in the Highlands."

Braheem looked questioningly at Gerald. Sometimes he could guess at the English lady's meaning, but not always.

"She says that your music reminds her and makes her long for the mountains of her homeland," translated Gerald obligingly.

Braheem smiled and stood up. Bowing a little and touching his finger to his forehead again, he explained that he must be going. Soon he was climbing the mountain away from them, whistling and calling to his scattered but active herd.

"Now let's go after the shovels and things!" suggested

Harry. Gerald and Boadie agreed with enthusiasm.

"How about you, Danny?" asked Gerald.

Danny looked at Miss Dunbar. "What are you going to do?" he inquired.

Miss Dunbar was folding up her campstool and setting it inside the cave.

"I am going to do a little reading," she replied. "Up in the big pine tree on the cliff. You may come along, if you like. — Though the tree itself isn't very good for climbing until your legs are longer."

"I'll look for a little tree near it," said Danny. "I think I'll go with Miss Dunbar. I haven't seen her climb trees yet," he ended gravely.

"Oh it's nothing," said Miss Dunbar modestly. "Come along then."

"We'll give you a shout when we're back," said Gerald. "So you can come and help us dig. Now, Harry and Boadie, we can take some of the picnic stuff back so we won't have so much to lug later."

Miss Dunbar and Danny left the others to gather up their loads, and started climbing toward the cliff. They did not talk much, but climbed steadily on until they had reached the foot of the old pine, stretching its branches out over the cliff. Here they stopped and rested. Far below them, they could hear Gerald's voice calling to Harry, and they looked to see how far the other three had gone.

Danny saw them first. "They're already at the house!" he exclaimed. "They must have run and slid all the way."

"It's a slower job going uphill," replied Miss Dunbar. "They're probably nearly ready to start back."

"They look so tiny, and yet we can understand every word they say!" said Danny.

"Yes, the air is very still and clear up here," said Miss Dunbar. "We can hear sounds from long distances. Besides, the children are standing right by the house, and that makes a sounding board. Their voices bounce off, you might say, and come back to us here. Listen."

Boadie's voice came, far away, but very clear, from a small blue dot by the house: "Don't talk rot! I may be a girl, but I'm going to carry my share. Give me that shovel."

Then Gerald's voice: "All right. I'll take the pickaxe and this hoe. Danny will be wanting to dig too."

Danny and Miss Dunbar exchanged a smile, and looked back to see that the three small dots had moved away from the house toward the thread of a path.

Presently Danny asked Miss Dunbar, "What was the name of that man — something like Useless?"

"Ulysses — the one I was telling you about?" replied Miss Dunbar gently.

"Yes," said Danny. "After all those years — did he look different when he came home? The minute he came in the door did his wife know who he was?"

"There was only one old friend who knew him when he came home," replied Miss Dunbar. "And that was his dog."

Danny's eyes brightened with interest. "Will you tell me about it, please? About the dog, I mean."

"The dog's name was Argos, and Ulysses took care of him when he was a puppy. When his master went away the dog still wasn't full grown, but he never forgot the man who had been kind to him. Well, twenty years later Ulysses returned to his home, on foot and weary. He was dressed in rags like a beggar. But as he entered the door he spoke to a swineherd there. An old dog lying near by picked up his ears and wagged his tail. It was Argos. He was too weak to move, and he was blind, but he heard the voice he loved."

Danny sat very still. Finally he asked, "Did Ulysses stop and pat him?"

"Naturally," Miss Dunbar assured him. "And faithful old

Argos never was parted from his master again."

Danny gave a deep sigh of satisfaction.

A call came up from below: "Danny!"

"Coming!" called Danny, scrambling to his feet. "They must be nearly there now." He hesitated. Miss Dunbar waited to see what he wanted; then suddenly she remembered.

"I'm going up in the tree right now," she asserted. "Usually when I'm by myself I take my shoes off first. It's much better climbing that way. You'll excuse me?"

"Of course," replied Danny politely, looking at her feet

and wondering how she kept her shoes so well polished with all this mountain climbing. His own small boots were very scuffed and dusty.

Miss Dunbar removed her oxfords and set them neatly together at the base of the tree. Then she went a few paces away from it. Here she turned and took two or three running steps and one big leap. As she leaped she grasped the lowest branch of the big pine and clung there. Her feet reached out and began walking up the trunk before Danny's fascinated gaze. Presently one trousered leg was over the branch and in a minute Miss Dunbar was on top of the branch, straddling it, and smiling down at Danny.

"It's quite simple really, you see," she explained. "Just a matter of practice, and keeping fit. Now you'd best go on down or they'll wonder what's happened to you. I shall go on up to the top and read some more about Ulysses." She proceeded to ascend the tree as Danny turned and started down, answering "Coming!" once more to a second impatient call from below.

He found the three adventurers in the midst of an argument in front of the cave entrance, on the subject of how the digging was to proceed.

Harry was of the opinion that each person should choose his own spot and just start digging — like wildcat prospectors in the West.

"It's more exciting that way," he said. "And as soon as anybody finds anything they can yell to the others."

"They'll yell all right, however we decide to dig," said Gerald. "But the point is we want to make a careful search, so we should do it the scientific way. We could all get in line at the back of the cave and dig a trench; then gradually work forward toward the opening. That way we won't miss anything — like real archaeologists."

"Arabic again?" inquired Boadie in a resigned tone.

"'Archaeologist' you mean?" said Gerald. "No, they're people who look for ancient buried cities and dig them up. We had one visiting us last winter and he told us how they do it. *First* they dig a trench!" He looked firmly at Harry.

"Prospecting is more fun," said Harry obstinately.

"Children dear, let's compromise!" suggested Boadie peaceably. "This cave is too small anyway for everybody to work in line. Our elbows would bump. Here's Danny now. He and Gerald and I can start with this — this — archangel's trench — while Harry works on some spot of his own."

"Right," said Harry. Gerald said nothing, but handed a hoe to Danny and crawled into the entrance carrying a pick. In a few moments the line which Boadie had suggested was starting a careful trench at the back of the cave, while Harry's wildcat mine was being opened up near the entrance.

"Just don't disturb the ants' nest," cautioned Danny. "They got here first."

"Don't try to dig hard or fast," warned Gerald. "You might strike something important and break it. It would really be best if we just used our hands to dig."

Boadie groaned. "Now he's telling us, after that long trip back to the house to get these things!"

"Well, after all, we couldn't dig up the whole cave floor with our bare hands," admitted Gerald.

He and Boadie had already started little holes, but Danny seemed to be having trouble. He wasn't one to give up easily though. When Gerald paused and looked over at him, Danny said, "I guess this hoe isn't a very good thing to dig with. Or maybe the ground is too hard here."

"I'll just start your hole for you," offered Gerald. He came over to Danny's side and Danny handed him the hoe.

But the first dig with the hoe made hardly any impression.

"You've struck a rock here," said Gerald, "or— !" His impressive pause brought Harry and Boadie over to peer over his shoulder as he knelt down and began brushing the thin layer of earth from whatever it was that was stopping the hoe.

"Of course it's probably just the rock floor of the cave," he said, but his quick eager work made his words unconvincing.

"There!" he said presently.

"Wow!" said Harry.

"What *is* it?" said Boadie.

"It looks like the top to a big pottery jar of some kind," said Gerald in an awed tone.

The three children were looking at a round jar cover of stone, with a rusty metal ring set in the top of it for lifting the heavy lid. Gerald felt around the lid, clearing the earth away with his fingers.

"There's a jar under it!" he said with excitement. "This is the top of a whole buried jar!"

"A jar! I never saw one as big as that!" said Boadie.

"We have them at home," said Gerald. "Ma uses them to keep olive oil in, or for storing olives."

"Open it!" said Boadie. "Hurry up!"

Gerald seemed suddenly reluctant.

"Well, I don't know," he said. "It's really not ours, you know."

Boadie fumed. "Honestly sometimes you boys are impossible! Whoever put it here is not coming back for it, and whatever it is in there is not going to bite us! Here, I'll open it myself." She kneeled down and put her hand on the metal ring. Then she stopped and said in a small voice, "Go on, Gerald, *you* open it."

Gerald laughed, and grasped the ring firmly to raise it. But the lid would not budge. He put both hands to the effort and tried again, but still there were no results.

"Either this lid is stuck on tight, or it's heavier than we thought," he remarked.

"Wait!" said Harry. "I'll get the broom and we'll slip the handle through the ring. Then two of us holding the ends of the broom handle can raise the lid."

"*Maybe,*" said Boadie pessimistically.

"Go ahead," said Gerald. "It's worth trying."

Harry ducked down through the entrance and emerged into the brilliant afternoon sunlight. He stood up and waited a moment blinking in the bright light and trying to remember where they had left the broom. Directly in front of him was the broad low window that "looked out on nothing." Framed in its large square he could see the inside of the house and could look right through the open front door to where the path wound around a shoulder of the hill just below the little house. A figure was coming up the path in his direction. Harry turned and dove back into the little cave.

"It's Edmund!" he gasped. "Lie low everybody!"

The other three joined Harry at the entrance, peering through the bush and listening. They could hear Edmund's footsteps clearly, but they could not see him from here.

"Oh dear!" whispered Boadie. "We shouldn't have left the matting and the broom out there. If he looks into the house he'll see them!"

"Sh!" said Gerald.

Edmund's steps paused a moment when he was near the little house but in a moment they could hear him continuing on up the path past it.

"It's a good thing," whispered Boadie, "that we didn't clear away all the thistles from that side. From the path it still just looks like a little old ruined house."

The footsteps had faded away on the mountain above them.

"Shall I sneak out and get the broom now?" asked Harry.

"Better wait a few minutes," said Gerald. "He may be sitting not far above here, or he might be coming back. We'll lie low for a bit. Did you see the broom anywhere?"

"No," said Harry. "I didn't even get into the house. I was standing just by the cave, sort of blinking in the sun. But I looked through the window — you know, the one Boadie says 'looks out on nothing.' And I saw him through the window, by looking clear through the house." Harry stopped as an idea struck him. "That's what that window is for! Not to look out of, but to look through from the *outside!* You can see the path perfectly and see if someone is coming!"

Boadie hopped up and danced with excitement. "And that explains why the house was built at this funny angle! Somebody wanted to use this cave to hide in, and the house was a good thing to hide behind and yet to peek through too, and — "

Gerald interrupted quietly. "But they lived in the house, and everybody knew they were here."

Harry and Boadie were silent, but Harry was still following his idea.

"Wait till we go out," he said. "You'll see what I mean. If you stand where I stood you can see the approach to the house *perfectly*. If the window were smaller, like the other windows, you couldn't; the window sill is just low enough to give a good view of the path, through the doorway."

Gerald looked at Harry thoughtfully; then he glanced back at the stone jar cover they had found.

"There's a lot that we don't know about this place," he said slowly. Then lowering his voice he added, "Do you know we've all been practically yelling in here. I hope Edmund isn't around."

Everyone fell silent, listening. Gerald moved to the entrance and peered out through the bush.

"I think he's gone," he said. "I don't hear anything — Wait! Yes, I do. Listen! He's coming back."

The others joined him in breathless silence at the entrance. Footsteps were coming down the mountain toward the ledge above them. Gerald crawled halfway out of the cave.

"Come back!" whispered Boadie.

"I'm being careful," whispered Gerald over his shoulder. Cautiously he raised his head and looked back up the mountain. Suddenly he ducked down again and into the cave.

"It's Edmund, all right," he murmured. "He's sitting on the ledge and he looks as if he were settled for the afternoon."

The four adventurers sat on the floor of the cave and looked at one another disconsolately. Through the hole above them they could hear Edmund moving around a little; then he seemed to settle down again. Through the hole they could hear him right over them whistling through his teeth. Boadie started to whisper something, but the boys silenced her with gestures. She turned and crawled over to the wall of the cave where Danny's knapsack still rested.

The boys watched her, and then their faces broke into grins as she returned carrying the empty vinegar bottle. She handed it to Gerald.

It took him a few moments to compose his features enough to blow into the bottle. First all he could produce was one feeble and brief little moan. The whistling above them stopped abruptly. Then Gerald blew again, and a

deep and resonant bass note moaned in the cave. The sound of hasty retreating footsteps told them that Edmund had left the ledge, and everybody rushed to the cave entrance. Gerald went out first, and beckoned to the rest. They all stood up, ready to retreat again if necessary, and watched as Edmund's back disappeared down the bit of path which they could see through the window of the old house.

"He won't bother us again today," said Gerald.

As his footsteps died away, Boadie remarked, "Well it's odd, isn't it, to build a window where the view is from the outside looking in, instead of the usual way."

"And if all these wild ideas are true," said Gerald slowly, "that would mean that the house was built right here because somebody knew the cave was here in the first place."

"Now I'll get the broom handle!" said Harry.

THE BROOM was leaning against the wall in the corner of the old house, where Boadie had left it, and in a moment the children were clustered around the jar top again while Harry kneeled down to fit the broom handle through the ring. But another disappointment met them here; the broom handle was just too wide, or the ring was just too small; the one would not go through the other. Harry sat back on his heels and looked at the others.

"How about your knife?" said Boadie, turning to Gerald. "Do you think you could whittle the handle down so it could go through?"

"I can try," said Gerald opening his knife. "I'll have to whittle quite a bit to do any good." He tested the blade on the broom handle, but it made hardly any impression on the hard polished wood.

"I'd have to work on it all night," he said gloomily, tossing the broom down. "And even then it might not work. The best thing is to get Pa up here and see if he can open it. We don't want to break the jar and spoil whatever is in it."

"I doubt if we could break it," said Harry. "Those big jars are pretty strong."

"What do you suppose is in it?" asked Boadie, sitting down cross-legged before the jar. "Maybe it's like Pandora's box, and we'll let out a lot of trouble if we open it."

"Don't be so dismal," said Gerald. "Maybe it's somebody's bones. Lots of ancient people buried their friends' bones in jars."

"And you're telling *me* not to be dismal!" exclaimed Boadie.

"Bones aren't dismal; they're interesting," said Gerald.

"Don't mind him; he's going to be a doctor someday," explained Harry. "Personally," he continued, "I think it's jewels. Or gold. Or maybe we'll find a very ancient and valuable piece of paper, with information that will change all of history."

"What do you think, Danny?" asked Boadie turning to him. "You've been very quiet."

"I think it might be somebody's collection," said Danny. "All the very best fossils he ever found. It would be a very safe place to keep them."

"Hush!" said Harry suddenly. Footsteps above them were coming slowly along the ledge.

"Not *again!*" whispered Boadie. "He's braver than I thought."

Gerald leaned over and picked up the vinegar bottle. He was not smiling now. "This time we'll scare him for good!" he said grimly.

Putting his lips to the bottle he blew two deep, moaning wails. Even Boadie shivered as she listened. The footsteps stopped, but they did not move away.

Presently a familiar voice remarked, "Very good, Vesuvius. And now do you children realize that it is nearly six o'clock?"

"Miss Dunbar!" called Boadie excitedly. "Do come down and see what we've found!"

In a moment Miss Dunbar was crawling into the cave.

"I hope it is worth all this trouble," she said. "I haven't had my tea, and I'm apt to be cross."

Boadie pointed out the jar top uncovered in the floor of the cave. Miss Dunbar raised her eyebrows and put her hand out to grasp the lid.

"My word, it must be heavy," she commented as she tried to lift it.

"We're going to bring Pa up here tomorrow," said Harry. "He'll open it for us. I suppose it's no use asking him to come up tonight."

"No, I suppose it's not," agreed Miss Dunbar sensibly. "And now could you tell me what the moaning was for?"

"We thought you were Edmund!" said Boadie. "Did it sound awful?"

"Horrible," said Miss Dunbar. "And why should I be Edmund?"

"We'll tell you what happened," said Boadie. As she explained the episode of Edmund's visit, the bewilderment on Miss Dunbar's face faded.

"And I thought Edmund was brave enough to come back," said Boadie in disgust. "I should have known better!"

"We forgot to have tea!" said Danny handing around the shoe box full of fruit.

"I like a man who keeps his mind on important issues," said Boadie, helping herself.

"I think if everybody carries something in one hand we can manage," said Miss Dunbar, "to walk down the mountain eating fruit with the other hand. We really must get home."

"Do get your lessons done fast tomorrow, Boadie," said

Gerald. "Harry and I'll start our studying tonight if we can. And tomorrow I know Pa will come up. He'll be as curious as we are about that jar."

A baffled and indignant meeting was being held under the clump of pines at the south end of the boys' house. Boadie and the boys had finished their studies early and Pa had promised to go up to the cave with them. And then just as they were ready to start up the path, callers had arrived.

"Why can't people come calling properly at tea time, and leave us the mornings to ourselves!" raged Boadie.

"You were a caller yourself yesterday morning," Harry pointed out.

"Who are these people anyway? Are they sick or something?" asked Boadie.

"No, they're not sick. And they're nice people," admitted Gerald. "It's just I wish they had come some other time."

"It's Sheikh Mohammed," explained Harry. "He's one of Pa's best friends, and we like him too. I don't know who's with him."

"Well, why don't you boys go in," said Boadie, "and tell your father that there's somebody here who's waiting to see the doctor? Then they'll leave."

"But there *isn't* anybody," objected Harry.

"Yes, there is," said Boadie. "*I'm* waiting to see him."

"Boadie, you haven't any principles," remarked Gerald.

"Not when I'm in a hurry," said Boadie. "Isn't there something you can do — in a high-principled sort of way?"

"We could go to the kitchen and help them hurry up

with the coffee. Guests aren't supposed to leave until the coffee has been served."

In a moment the morning peace of the kitchen was shattered by the appearance of three whirlwinds at the door.

"We've come to help!" said Gerald. "Harry, you get the tray and show Boadie where the coffee cups are. Fitny," he said, turning to the transfixed cook, "put the coffee in the grinder and I'll grind it for you. Do hurry!"

"In the name of Heaven!" exclaimed Fitny in a bewildered tone. "What's happened? Is someone hurt?"

"I can't find the coffee," said Gerald, moving a row of cans and packages and paper bags from the cupboard to the kitchen table. "We're helping you, Fitny, that's all." He peered into a paper bag and finding some sticks of cinnamon bark, put one in his mouth as he continued his search. The paper bag joined the growing line on the table.

"The Lord give me grace!" implored Fitny. "Please put those things back. If you want coffee, dear, just tell me and I'll make you some. I didn't know your mother liked you to — oh dear Heaven!" she exclaimed as Harry entered the kitchen and set down a tray with three small coffee cups and saucers. Boadie followed with a plate of little cakes.

"Those cakes are for the tea this afternoon! And those are your mother's best cups!" In despair she fled from the kitchen.

"What's the matter with her?" asked Boadie. "She looked upset. I wish I knew Arabic."

"Arabic wouldn't help," replied Harry. "I don't know what's the matter with her either. Gerald, do we need all that stuff to make coffee?"

By now Gerald had the contents of two shelves set out on

the table which was beginning to look pretty well covered.
As he dove down to start on the third shelf he did not reply.

"Are you going to make a cake?" asked Harry. "That'll
take forever."

Gerald emerged, rather crossly. "I am *not* making a cake.

I don't know *where* she keeps the coffee," he said.

"This smells like coffee over here," said Boadie, picking a bag up off the stove.

At this point their mother came into the kitchen, with Fitny's face peering wildly over her shoulder.

"Now what's going on in here, children?" she asked mildly.

"We're helping Fitny," said Harry.

"You're driving her crazy," remarked Ma.

"We want her to get the coffee in to the visitors as fast as she can, so they'll go and we can get up to the cave," explained Gerald.

"Well, she'll do it a lot faster by herself," said Ma. "Harry and Boadie, you'd better go and wait somewhere else. Gerald, please put those things back in the cupboard where you found them."

Gerald turned toward the cupboard, but Fitny flew over to it ahead of him muttering what sounded like a prayer of some kind, and stood guard in front of it.

"All right, Gerald," said his mother. "I think Fitny would rather do it herself. You can go on with the others. If you want to help another time, please ask me about it first."

" — So we're back where we were," muttered Boadie glumly when they were under the pines again. "We just wasted our valuable time."

"Well, the coffee will be in soon now," said Harry.

"I think you boys should go in and say good morning to the callers, anyway," said Boadie.

"What good would that do?" Gerald inquired.

"Not much," admitted Boadie. "But on the other hand, it might. One of the visitors might ask you, 'And what are you boys doing today?' Then you would have a chance to

say, 'Our father is taking us for a walk as soon as he's free.'
Sort of a hint you see."

"Sort of," agreed Gerald.

"I'll listen outside the window," said Boadie. "Good
luck!"

Fitny stood just inside the door waiting with the tray in
her hands. As the boys appeared at the door a little moan
escaped her, and her resigned expression drooped even
lower. The men paused in their conversation and looked up.

"Come in, boys," said Pa. "Sheikh Mohammed has brought
a friend to call on us." The boys walked over first and shook
hands with the Sheikh; their father introduced them to the
other gentleman.

"This is Mr. Haddad, from Beirut. He hasn't been well,
so he has come to Shemlan for a few days' rest. He is staying at the Sheikh's."

The boys murmured politely, smiling at the tall gentleman with the thin, tired face. He was dressed in a Western
business suit, but on his head, like Sheikh Mohammed, he
wore a red fez with a black tassel. Sheikh Mohammed as
usual wore his long straight-cut robe, though on top of it
was an ordinary suit coat. His handsome brown face was
smiling at the boys and his eyes twinkled as he asked in
Arabic, "Have you been working on your baseball field this
year, Gerald?"

Gerald grinned a little sheepishly. "Not much," he said.
"We've been spending a lot of time on the mountain."
Sheikh Mohammed liked to tease the boys about what slow
workers they were. Last summer they had started work on
a wheat field north of the house which they intended to
level off into a baseball diamond. Somehow the work had
gone very slowly.

Mr. Haddad smiled and remarked, "It's a pity to spend all your vacation working." Then he added in English, "So you are playing baseball this morning?"

"Oh — I guess we'll go up on the mountain," said Gerald. Harry thought he heard a snort from outside the window.

"Excuse us, please. We have a friend waiting outside," explained Gerald.

They made a hurried exit under the baleful eye of Fitny. Their friend who was waiting outside greeted them with disdain.

"What a chance! You muffed it completely," said Boadie. "He even *asked* you what you were doing today."

"Well, you needn't have snorted so loud," said Harry with dignity.

"Now we'll just have to wait," said Boadie.

But it seemed that at last the visit had come to an end. The voices of the men were moving from the parlor, and soon they heard polite farewells outside the house. The three children sprang to action.

"I'll go find Danny," said Boadie starting toward the back door. "And you boys see if you can persuade your mother to come along."

"Too bad Miss Dunbar isn't with us for this," commented Harry.

"She's sorry to miss it too," said Boadie. "Only she said it was too good an opportunity for her to go to Souk and get some errands done — knowing your father would be along to chaperon me in the presence of you ruffians." She disappeared into the house, calling Danny, and the boys followed.

Some twenty minutes later, it was a tense and quiet group that gathered around the scraped-off place in the floor of Danny's cave. Ma and Pa were both there, and

John too, who had protestingly ridden up part of the way on Pa's back.

"But I can walk perfickly," he argued.

"I know you can, old scout," replied his father. "This is just so we'll get there faster."

"I wouldn't miss this for anything," Ma had replied when the boys urged her to come. She had no "divided skirt" like Miss Dunbar's, but she had worn her old khaki hiking skirt and crawled into the cave as quickly as anybody.

Pa was kneeling down now, and feeling in the earth under the edges of the jar lid as Gerald had done before.

"You're right," said he. "There seems to be a large jar underneath this thing, buried in the earth."

"Is it ancient, do you think?" inquired Harry.

"Don't know. Looks just like a plain old modern one to me," replied his father. "Curious."

He stood up right over the lid, planting a foot on each side of it to brace himself; then bending over he put one hand under each edge and heaved. The lid came off and at once seven heads bumped as everybody tried to look in at once.

"It's so dark I can't see a thing in there!" said Harry.

"I can only see all my family's heads!" complained John who had gotten there last.

"Stand back, everybody," ordered Pa. "Now we will each have a chance for a good look, one at a time, before we disturb anything." He pulled a small flashlight out of his pocket and handed it to Ma. "Ladies first," he said. "You next, Dorothy. And you boys line up behind. I'll come last so I can take my time."

Everybody watched Ma's face as she bent over and looked

into the jar. She had a puzzled expression. Then she handed the flashlight to Boadie and stepped back.

"What is it, Ma?" asked Harry. "It isn't empty, is it?"

"Oh no," said his mother. "There seem to be several things in there."

Boadie was stepping back from the jar now to make way for Danny and John, who came together. She too looked somewhat puzzled and made a little face. Danny looked

in and remarked simply, "No fossils. Too bad."

John leaned over the jar and blew into it. He did not seem to think much of it.

Harry took the flashlight and looked in. "Hum," he said thoughtfully, and stepped aside for Gerald.

"I never saw such an inarticulate group," said their father. "Is this what you call scientific reporting?"

Gerald made an effort. "It looks to me like a lot of junk that nobody would want," he said.

Now his father was peering in. "I see what you mean," he said. "Let's start taking the stuff out so we can examine it."

First he lifted out a man's rough walking shoe, of the type that the mountaineers wore, with heavy nails in the sole and a pointed toe which curled up a little in front.

"Here's the other," he said, setting a second one beside the first. Next he pulled out a little bottle which seemed to have a small amount of gummy stuff still inside it. He sniffed it and made a face.

"Olive oil, would you say?" he asked handing it to Ma. She smelled it too, distastefully.

"It might have been once," she replied.

The next object he pulled out was a rusty lantern. The end of a small candle was still stuck in it. Under this was a piece of rolled up material. After Pa had lifted it up and shaken it out, it proved to be a man's coat, of fairly ordinary style but moldy and musty smelling.

"See if there's anything in the pockets," Pa said, handing it to Gerald. Gerald investigated thoroughly.

"Nothing at all," he reported.

"We're getting near the bottom," remarked Pa. "Here's something pretty messy." He pulled out what appeared to be a hard mass of something that had once been moldy, but had now turned black and hard. He laid it on the ground.

"It might have been Arab bread," remarked Ma, turning it over with her foot.

"And that's all," announced Pa.

"Aw!" A disappointed chorus greeted him.

"I'm sorry," said Pa. "Take a look yourselves." One by one the children looked into the empty jar.

"But who do you suppose put that stuff in there so carefully?" asked Boadie. "And *why?*"

"Well, I wouldn't say it was put there so carefully," replied Pa. "It looked to me more as if it had been dumped in. And as for *why* — I wish I knew. Maybe we'll never know."

A sudden deep groan made them all jump.

"Danny, put that thing down!" said Gerald. Danny looked up happily from the vinegar bottle.

"I made it work!" he said. "Listen to me!" He blew another groaning note in the bottle.

"That's how we scared Edmund away," he said to his parents.

"It's enough to scare anybody," remarked his father. "What was this about Edmund?"

Gerald explained. "I don't see why we have to be always running away from that guy," he ended. "What a pest!"

"You don't have to," his father assured him calmly.

"But we don't want him nosing into everything we do," said Gerald. "What's the matter with his parents anyway? Why don't they take care of him?"

"Are you complaining, or do you really want to know?" asked his father.

A little surprised, Gerald replied, "I really want to know."

"Well," said Pa, "his own father is dead. A few years ago

his mother married again. I think Edmund did not approve of the marriage."

"Oh," said Gerald. The children's silence was full of sympathy.

"Is his stepfather cruel to him?" asked Harry.

"From what I've seen I gather it's the other way round," said Pa a little dryly. "He's cruel to his stepfather. At least, that's what my hunch is. His stepfather seems to spend most of his time away from home on business trips."

"I don't blame him!" said Boadie heartily.

"Now what are we going to do with these exhibits?" asked Ma, with a housewife's instinct for order.

"Let's put them back in the jar for the time being," suggested Pa. "Have you children excavated the rest of this cave yet?"

"No," said Harry. "We were just starting when Danny's hoe hit on this thing."

"Let's have the hoe," said Pa. Harry handed it to him. Dragging the hoe across the floor of the cave, Pa made a shallow trench. Then he drew another parallel to the first and another and another until he had furrowed the entire floor of the cave in a few minutes.

"Well there's nothing else here as shallowly buried as the jar was anyway," he remarked. "Now let's each take a hoe or shovel or whatever you've got here and make each trench deeper, working side by side."

There were only four tools to dig with, so Ma and Danny were commissioned to watch the dug-up places to see that nothing was missed. John decided to dig a trench of his own outside, where there was more room. The trenches grew deeper fast.

Pa stood up and wiped his forehead.

"As for Edmund," he said. "With someone like that there are only two things you can do. First, you can ignore him. Or second, if he won't let you ignore him, you can take him in hand. Nobody's hopeless."

"Edmund is," replied Boadie promptly. "If you'll pardon my saying so," she added politely.

"Nobody is hopeless," repeated Pa blandly. "Find out what's ailing him."

"What Edmund needs," said Boadie, "is a good English governess."

"What he needs," remarked Pa quietly, "is a real friend."

The boys were silent, digging away. But Boadie said, a little defiantly, "Well in my opinion it's the puppy that needs a real friend."

The digging went on in silence. But the work seemed to go fast, and at last the whole floor of the little cave had been explored, with no further discoveries.

"That's all for today," said Pa looking at his watch.

"I must go down and get some things done; it'll soon be lunch time," said Ma.

"I'll go with you," said Pa. "Come on, John. Show us how you can walk down all the way. You boys might smooth down the floor of the cave again to make it a pleasant place to sit. It's cool in here. But don't forget to come to lunch when we call."

Gerald and Harry started restoring the floor of the cave as their parents walked down the hill.

"I'll help you in a minute," said Boadie, and went out to look for Danny. He was sitting on the matting in the little house watching a hornet eat a crumb of samboosic left from the picnic the day before. In a minute she was back in the cave.

"What's Danny doing?" asked Gerald.

"Watching a hornet clean up after our picnic," said Boadie briefly, patting down the earth with the back of the shovel.

"Those hornets are getting worse," said Gerald. "They're eating up the grapes in the vineyard. It's time we went after them."

"How about a hornet hunt this afternoon?" suggested Harry.

"A *hornet* hunt?" asked Boadie. "How would that do any good — shooting a few hornets?"

Gerald and Harry shouted with laughter. "We don't *shoot* them," said Harry. "We use tennis racquets. Old ones. And we get the whole nest. It's very exciting."

"How do you do it?" asked Boadie.

"First you go into the vineyard," said Gerald, "to a spot where the grapes are sweetest and ripest."

"Sounds like a pleasant way to begin!" murmured Boadie.

"Then you choose a hornet," began Harry.

"Watch him when he finishes with a grape and sails away," went on Gerald.

"Follow him!" added Harry with rising excitement.

"Jump the terraces! Leap over any stone walls in the way!" yelled Gerald.

"Don't let him get out of sight!" roared Harry joyously.

"But he does, of course," said Gerald with a sigh. "They nearly always do."

"Never mind!" Harry reassured Boadie. "Just remember the line he went in."

"Now go back to the vineyard!" Gerald entreated her solemnly.

"To a different part of it of course," added Harry. "As far away as possible from the first place."

"Choose another hornet!" implored Gerald.

"Watch him when he starts off!" cautioned Harry.

"Chase him!" broke in Boadie excitedly, getting into the spirit of the thing.

"Of course!" yelled Harry. "Up the mountain or down the terraces!"

"Don't lose him!" Boadie yelled back, dancing up and down.

"You've got the idea!" said Gerald happily.

"Till you fall flat on your face," ended Boadie.

"Right! — Who's explaining this, anyway?" demanded Gerald.

"*But,*" said Harry impressively, "remember the line he went in."

"This all sounds like a lot of fun. For the hornet," said Boadie.

"We're only beginning," said Gerald. "Now you've got two lines starting from different places in the vineyard. Continue those lines out over the countryside and somewhere they'll cross. AT THAT POINT — you will find your hornets' nest."

"Not I," said Boadie. "You can have mine."

"Stop interrupting. When you've found the hole in the ground where their nest is," continued Gerald, "you pour a lot of dirt on it. Then stand by with your tennis racquet ready. When the first hornet comes crawling out — "

"Whack him!" yelled Harry.

"But keep watching for outsiders that might be returning to the hole. Whack them too!"

"And then when your back's turned," warned Harry, "suddenly three or four crawl out of the hole at once!"

"Whack 'em!" yelled Boadie and Gerald in chorus.

"It gets pretty exciting when you're in the thick of it," admitted Harry happily.

"Does this go on all night?" inquired Boadie.

Gerald shook his head. "After a while the hornets stop coming out of the hole and you know you've got them — all except the grubs and the queen. Then you dig up the nest and burn it. You can collect the queen and take her home in a bottle if you find her. Hornet queens are rather unusual."

Boadie shook her head slowly. "So that's what you plan to do this afternoon?"

"Yes. Come on! We've got an old racquet for you and you know you can run like fury," urged Gerald handsomely.

"No thanks," said Boadie. "Hornet hunts aren't for me. You tell me about it afterwards. I think Danny and I'll go for a walk instead."

"Where?" asked the boys together.

"Just around," said Boadie vaguely. "But not anywhere near the vineyard, I can promise you that. I wouldn't want to be caught in any line that your hornet might be taking."

The boys used all their arts of persuasion, even offering her the queen hornet for her own, but Boadie was not to be moved. Hornet hunting was not for her, and she was going to take a walk with Danny.

At the supper table that night the story of the hornet hunt was re-enacted. It had been a highly successful afternoon. Two nests had been destroyed, and the glory of the day was not dimmed by the fact that one of Harry's eyes was almost closed by an enormous sting.

"They were coming too fast," he explained. "Three came out at once and Gerald couldn't help me because he was getting one that was coming from the other direction."

After supper Harry followed Gerald on to the balcony.

"Didn't you think Danny was sort of quiet at supper?" he asked.

"Probably had his mouth full," replied Gerald. "Besides,

he didn't have much chance to say anything," he added pointedly.

Harry ignored the brotherly comment, and continued meditatively, "I was wondering if he was worried about anything. Usually he's so interested in what's going on, but tonight he didn't seem to pay much attention to what we were saying."

"Oh he's probably tired — all the excitement in the cave this morning, and then the hike this afternoon."

"That's probably it," said Harry.

It HAD BEEN Boadie's suggestion, the following morning, that they go to Slanty Rocks instead of the ruined house.

"I told Miss Dunbar about the Rocks and she's dying to see them."

"Am I?" inquired Miss Dunbar raising her eyebrows slightly.

"You would find them interesting geologically," said Harry.

"To say nothing of the wild life there. That's where we found Boadie," explained Gerald. "In a jackal hole. Odd place for a girl."

"Can Danny come too?" asked Boadie. "We won't go if it's too far for him."

"He's been hiking so much this year I'm sure he could go. But we'll ask Ma."

So permission had been obtained, and the expedition was a success. Miss Dunbar and Danny had been introduced to the ironing-board rock and the jackal hole and the balcony rock. Danny had even contributed his wisp of hair to the others in the aspirin box. Miss Dunbar had been invited to, but she declined.

"Save the honor for the men and women of the future like yourselves," she said. "I'm already in my prime."

And now the older boys and Boadie wanted to go on and explore the rocks a little further.

"Will you come too?" they asked the others.

"No thank you," said Miss Dunbar. "I've nearly finished my book and I think I'll walk back along the path a little way to the pine tree. I'll sit in the shade there and finish reading it."

"In the tree or under it?" asked Danny.

"Under it," said Miss Dunbar. "Then when I'm finished I can lie down a bit and think."

"I think I'll come with you," said Danny. "I'm a little tired of being boosted around over these rocks. Some of them scratch your stomach and legs when you get dragged up the sides of them. But I'm glad I came, and thanks for dragging and boosting me," he said politely to his brothers.

"I'll blow my police whistle when it's time to start down," said Miss Dunbar.

In a few minutes she and Danny were walking along the little path around the shoulder of the mountain.

"Do you always carry that little box of medicine and stuff wherever you go?" asked Danny.

"Always on an expedition," said Miss Dunbar.

"Why?" asked Danny.

"Just to be prepared," was the reply. "In case anything happens."

"I'm prepared too," said Danny shyly. "Look."

Miss Dunbar stopped in the path and turned around. Danny was taking off his little knapsack. Laying it on the ground he took out of it a small tin box which said "Huyler's DeLuxe Candy." He handed it to Miss Dunbar and invited her to open it. This she did, and inside she found a little roll of gauze, a piece of cotton, and a small pair of gold embroidery scissors.

"Pa gave me the cotton and gauze," he said proudly.

"And your mother gave you the scissors?"

"Not exactly," admitted Danny. "I borrowed them. She was busy talking to Fitny. But I'll give them back to her as soon as we get home."

"You'd better," advised Miss Dunbar. "Now put the box away. We'll call on you if we need it."

"Who was that?" asked Danny suddenly, looking up the path behind Miss Dunbar.

Miss Dunbar turned. "I don't see anybody."

"I thought I saw somebody ahead of us just going around that turn."

"Well, they're probably way ahead of us now. Pick up your knapsack and we'll go along."

"I used to think I might be a scientist," said Danny as they started along the path again; "but now I think I might be a doctor someday. Like Gel."

"Well, there's time to think it over yet," said Miss Dunbar. "And here we are at the pine."

"I brought a book too," said Danny. "I can't read much, except my own name, but I like pictures."

Soon they were settled with their backs against the tree, Miss Dunbar reading the *Odyssey* and Danny with his copy of the *National Geographic Magazine*. Bees hummed near them in the heather and the breeze whispered in the pine needles above their heads. Suddenly Danny jumped.

"Something hit my page!" he said. "A little stone or something hit it hard!"

Miss Dunbar looked around. "There's nobody here. It must have been a bee or some insect that flew against it."

"It might have been," said Danny. "But it scared me." He moved a little closer to Miss Dunbar and they started reading again.

Soon Danny jumped up. "A lot of people are coming!" he

said. "I hear them!" He ran down the mountain a little way, and called back, "It's the goats!"

In a minute the flock began to appear here and there, and then in a black mass, all jumping and leaping and making snorting noises as they covered the rocks. Presently Braheem's smiling brown face appeared as he rounded the shoulder of the mountain.

"Marhaba!" called Danny happily.

"Marhabtain!" replied Braheem cheerfully. Then catching sight of Miss Dunbar he called out, "Marhaba, ya Sitt Miss Dumba!"

Miss Dunbar removed her eyeglasses. "Marhabtain, Braheem, my boy," she replied. "How is your finger today?"

Braheem walked over to where she was sitting, squatted down near her and held up his thumb for inspection. The bandage was off it, and the thumb was beginning to heal. After Miss Dunbar had inspected it, Braheem pulled a small flat newspaper package out of some inner pocket and handed it to her. A little surprised, Miss Dunbar opened it to find the gauze bandage which had been washed and ironed and carefully folded up. "Why, thank you!" said Miss Dunbar. "You needn't have bothered!"

But Braheem was smiling and pointing under the little bandage. Miss Dunbar raised it and found under it a little lace needlework doily.

"For Sitt Miss Dumba," said Braheem in Arabic. "From my mama."

"Oh please tell her that I thank her very much! Did she make this?" asked Miss Dunbar.

Braheem looked at Danny.

"Did your mother make it?" asked Danny.

"Yes," Braheem nodded proudly. "She said I must bring this to the lady doctor."

"He thinks you're a doctor," said Danny, "and I don't know how to say governess in Arabic. In fact," he added honestly, "I really don't know what it is in English. You're my first example of one."

"Well, keep it until you get a better one," quoted Miss Dunbar slyly. Danny grinned. Braheem smiled too, companionably.

"You Danny," said Braheem, "are you reading a book too? Can you read?"

Danny glanced down at the magazine which was still in his hand.

"Not really," he admitted. "This book has lots of pictures. Look." The two boys squatted down together under the tree with the magazine.

A shriek from one of the goats interrupted them. Braheem leaped to his feet. One of the goats was rushing madly down the hillside. Suddenly another one very near them gave a leap into the air and began running wildly in another direction. Braheem yelled at them and whistled. A third one gave a yell and seemed to go mad.

"In the name of all that's holy!" exclaimed Braheem. "Have they all gone crazy?" He was running distractedly up the hill trying to collect the goats while Danny ran down the hill to head off one that seemed to be making for Beirut. Miss Dunbar, still seated under the tree, had laid aside her book and was studying the situation. The behavior of the goats was very puzzling. Suddenly something bounced off her hat and landed in her lap. She picked it up in her fingers. It was a small stone. A thought began to dawn on her. Rising from the ground she walked back a little way from the tree and looked up. Just over where she had been sitting, among the lower branches, a boy was grinning at her. She called Danny over and nodded toward the boy.

"Do you know who that is?" she asked.

"Oh yes," said Danny without enthusiasm. "That's Edmund."

"Edmund," called Miss Dunbar. "Please come out of that tree directly and put away that slingshot."

Edmund's only answer was to aim at a hapless goat that was passing. The goat leaped up in the air when the stone hit it, and ran off.

"That's a very dangerous game," said Miss Dunbar. "You could blind one of the animals — let alone the people. And you're making a lot of trouble for the boy who's in charge."

Edmund shot at another goat. There was no doubt that he had a very good aim.

"I would advise you to come down out of that tree," said Miss Dunbar.

Edmund laughed. Miss Dunbar stooped down and neatly removed her oxfords as Danny watched, fascinated.

Then everything happened so fast that the next few minutes were rather confused. Braheem, returning with a wandering goat, was bewildered to see a whirl of flying brown trousers which passed him and flashed up the tree trunk. Edmund, for a moment transfixed with surprise, suddenly started retreating up into the higher branches. The apparition followed him and caught up with him easily. Edmund shrank back cowering against the tree trunk, his eyes wide with terror. Miss Dunbar, balancing easily on the tree, with one hand on the branch above her, held out her other hand.

"Give me the slingshot please."

Edmund handed her the slingshot.

"Don't look like that. I am not going to throw you over the cliff."

An admiring murmur rose from below, in Arabic.

"May the name of God be upon her! What a lady!"

Edmund said nothing.

"Now come right down from the tree and apologize to that young Arab."

Edmund turned and began climbing down obediently. He and Miss Dunbar dropped to the ground simultaneously. Braheem recognized him and stepped back a little way cautiously.

"Poor fellow," he said pityingly, touching his head.

Miss Dunbar saw the gesture and spoke rather sharply. "There's nothing wrong with his head. He simply needs to learn a few things. Apologize to the young man, Edmund."

"Sorry," muttered Edmund.

"Not very good, but you're probably out of practice," said Miss Dunbar briskly. "Translate his apology please, Danny."

Danny did his best. Braheem assured them all that it had been no trouble, none of the goats were hurt, praise the Lord, and boys would be boys, and the young American was just having fun. Then with a good-natured grin he made his farewell salaams and called the goats together. Soon he was over the ridge and they could hear his pipes playing in the distance.

Miss Dunbar turned to Edmund who was still standing before her, morosely staring at the toe of his shoe.

"That's that," said she. "Now brace up and stop looking as if we were going to eat you. — You use a very awkward technique in climbing, you know. I don't see how you ever got up into the tree to start with."

Edmund looked up with some astonishment into the clear gray eyes that were looking mildly at him. He saw no unfriendliness there.

"I — I just climbed," he said.

"Let me see how you go up," she ordered. "That lowest branch is a long way from the ground."

Edmund walked over to the tree and grasping the trunk with his arms he shinnied slowly and painfully up. He had two or three false starts, but eventually he was up on the first branch.

"Very well, you did it," said Miss Dunbar. "A bit awkward that, though. Your arms are probably all scratched up. Now come down and I'll show you the proper technique."

She explained about the shoes and then demonstrated the flying-jump technique of grasping the lowest branch and walking up the tree as you hang from the branch. When one leg was over the branch she paused, dangling head down, and explained: "This requires a certain amount of height, but you are a well-grown boy, quite tall, really." She dropped to the ground again and continued the lecture. "A bit fat though," said she tapping Edmund's belt with the back of her fingers. "Lose a little of that and you'll feel more fit. Too many sweets and puddings, no doubt."

She sat down to put on her shoes.

"A little practice, that's all. And a little dieting. See what you can do. You may go now," she concluded as if she were dismissing him from the schoolroom. Edmund murmured, "Goodbye," and started home down the hill. The astonished look had not faded from his face.

Miss Dunbar rose, picked up her book and turned to Danny.

"And now we'll go around the mountain a little way and blow the whistle," she said. "It's time to be going home."

The whistle's blast brought an answering sound from Slanty Rocks, something which sounded like a jackal's howl. Soon after, three figures appeared in the distance.

When the three had caught up with Miss Dunbar and Danny they all started down the hill. Gerald and Danny were the last in line on the path.

"Did you get very tired waiting for us under the tree?" asked Gerald. "Was it boring?"

"No, not boring at all," said Danny. "It was quite interesting."

"You're a good sport, Danny," said Boadie who was walking just ahead of them and had heard the interchange. "How would you like to come to my house this afternoon for tea?"

"Just me?" asked Danny.

"Just you," said Boadie.

"I'll ask my mother," said Danny, his face red with pleasure. "I'd like to come very much."

Tea was nearly over.

"Why can't we have this chocolate cake for tea every day?" asked Harry scraping the last bit of frosting off his plate.

Before his mother could answer, Fitny appeared at the back door.

"There's a lady who wants to see you," she said. "And she has her son with her."

"Bring them out here," said Ma, rising. "And Fitny, please bring us a fresh pot of tea — Why, Mrs. Bixton, how nice!" she said in English, as the lady appeared behind Fitny.

Mrs. Bixton seemed to be agitated.

"Pardon my walking right out here," she said. "I couldn't understand your maid, so I just followed where she led me."

"Sit right down here and have some tea," said Ma. "How do you do, Edmund."

"Oh, no tea, please, thanks. I couldn't. How do you do, Doctor. This is very distressing! I hardly know how to begin."

"Our dog has been stolen," said Edmund bluntly. He was still standing in the doorway, his hands in his pockets.

His mother turned to him. "Edmund, you promised!" Then she turned back to her hostess. "Our puppy has disappeared, and Edmund is so worried about him. He insisted that we come here. He thought that you people, knowing the village so well and all, might be able to suggest something — "

Ma began to murmur sympathetically, but Edmund interrupted her. "You know perfectly well why I made you come here, Mother."

His mother flushed. "Oh Edmund, please!"

Edmund continued: "Gerald and Harry stole the dog. They wanted him in the first place and I told them they couldn't have him. They've been rude and mean every time I've seen them and now they've taken my dog."

Gerald and Harry stared at him in open astonishment. Their father gave them only a glance and then looked steadily at Edmund. Mrs. Bixton was staring into her lap, where her hands were busily folding her handkerchief up into a tight wad.

"I don't know *what* to say to you," she murmured. "He has this fixed idea!"

Edmund's lip was beginning to tremble and his eyes filled with tears as he began to yell at the boys, "You took him! You took him! He's my property and I want him back! I hate you!"

Pa stood up and walked over to Edmund. "Edmund!" he said sternly. "Stop that this minute! Control yourself."

Edmund's mother pleaded, "Oh Doctor, please. He's so upset over this."

Pa paid no attention to the lady. "Stop it instantly!" he

said. Edmund stopped his sobbing and looked sullenly at him with his eyes full of tears.

"That's better," said Pa. "Now suppose you sit down over here and we'll talk this over quietly."

After they were both seated, he addressed himself again to Edmund.

"Edmund, you do really believe our boys took your dog, don't you?" He turned to Gerald and Harry. "Boys, did you take Edmund's dog, under some mistaken idea that it was your duty to rescue it?"

"No, we did not!" said Gerald firmly and looked at Harry who shook his head.

"I thought not," said their father. "Now Edmund, what makes you think this puppy was stolen? Maybe he just ran away. From reports I've heard, I understand you have given him rather severe treatment."

Edmund flushed at this last remark. "He couldn't have run away," he replied. "I kept him always in the back yard surrounded by a high stone wall. Somebody climbed over that stone wall and took him." He glared at Gerald and Harry.

"How old is the puppy and what does he look like?"

Edmund described him.

"Was he a valuable breed of dog? A good hunting dog or anything?"

"No," said Edmund. "I think he was part fox terrier."

"Seems unlikely anybody would steal him around here," remarked Pa meditatively. "Most dogs aren't very highly thought of, unless they're hunting dogs."

"He's a little pup," chimed in Gerald worriedly. "If he's lost he can't take care of himself very well."

Edmund looked up at Gerald; for the first time a look of doubt was in his eyes.

"When did you first miss him?" asked Harry.

"This afternoon," said Edmund. "I went out to see him and the cook said he was gone. But he may have been gone all night. The cook couldn't find him this morning, but she was scared to tell me."

"He was there last night though?" asked Gerald. "When did you feed him yesterday?"

Edmund looked a little sullen. "I didn't feed him. The cook does that."

Gerald looked disgusted. "So he may have been gone yesterday for all you know — Or care," he added under his breath.

"Well," said his father, "we can tell some of our village friends about him and ask them to keep an eye out for him. Some of the children might have seen him around. It's hard to hide a dog very long — even a puppy."

"Sometimes if a dog is injured," said Gerald, "he will crawl into some hole and hide. He might even be around your house somewhere. Look, Edmund, Harry and I'll come home with you right now and help you look around."

Mrs. Bixton's face brightened and Edmund looked both surprised and pleased. Fitny had brought in the pot of fresh tea and now Mrs. Bixton consented to stay and have a cup. But the boys were impatient to get started.

"We'll go on ahead," said Gerald.

"At least have a piece of this chocolate cake to eat as you go," said Ma to Edmund. He cast one interested glance at it, hesitated, then to everyone's astonishment he said, "Thanks but not just now." He tightened his belt a little and followed Gerald and Harry around the house.

About an hour later, Gerald and Harry were walking dejectedly back from Edmund's house.

"At least we found out one thing," said Harry. "It was possible for the puppy to get out of that yard if he wanted to. Edmund didn't even know there was that hole there."

"If I could just be sure that the pup was not hurt or anything, I'd be glad he'd escaped," commented Gerald. "It's just that a little puppy can get into so much trouble."

"I know it," said Harry glumly.

In a moment Gerald broke the silence again. "Do you know that I think Edmund really misses that puppy now that he's gone?"

"Sure," said Harry a little sourly; "he hasn't got anything to kick around any more."

"That may be partly it," conceded Gerald. "But he really worked hard looking for him. Crawling in around that black hole behind the cistern under the house. I think he may be a little ashamed of the way he treated the pup."

"Hm," said Harry, noncommittally.

There was another silence. Then Gerald glanced at Harry and said cautiously, "You don't suppose that Boadie and Danny — " He left the sentence unfinished, but Harry understood.

"I thought of that too," he replied. "Boadie might, but I don't think Danny would. — Still, she's a smart persuader," he ended uncomfortably.

They were nearing the little short cut that led up to their house from the road.

"We'll ask Boadie," said Gerald with decision. "But not in front of Danny. He'd just feel badly about the pup being lost — if he doesn't know anything about it," he ended a little ambiguously.

They climbed the hill and walked around the house to the back porch. Here they sat on the back of the stone seats, swinging their legs.

"I wonder how soon Danny'll be back from Boadie's," said Gerald.

But it was not from the direction of Boadie's house that their brother finally appeared with his hostess. The boys suddenly saw them strolling down through the vineyard, from the direction of the ruined house. Danny saw them and waved.

"We went for a walk after tea!" he called.

As they drew near, Gerald said to Danny, "Pa and Ma are invited out to dinner tonight. If you want to see them before they go, better go on in."

"All right," said Danny cheerfully. " 'Bye, Boadie, and thanks!" With a wave to them all he went inside.

"I must be getting home too," remarked Boadie.

"Just a minute," said Gerald. "We want to ask you something. Do you know anything about Bouncy, the Bixtons' puppy?"

Boadie looked off at the mountain a moment; then she turned around and faced him squarely. "Bouncy ran away, all by himself," she said. "When we found him outside the wall, of course we had to take care of him."

"Do you mean to say Danny is in on this?" asked Gerald.

"We both found him together," said Boadie defiantly.

Gerald was very angry. "It's bad enough if you want to twist things around and pretend that black is white, but if you're going to take other people's property I wish you wouldn't drag my little brother into it."

"Gerald, my dear fellow," said Boadie with a supreme effort at self-control, "I wish that once — just once — you could forget that New England conscience of yours."

"You can be very funny sometimes, Boadie," rejoined Gerald. "But this time you'd better be serious."

"Well, I am serious," said Boadie, her face white and set. "And I want you to know I have a conscience too. A British one. It may be different from yours, but it's just as cast-iron strong as your New England conscience. And my conscience won't allow me to let an innocent puppy suffer — I don't care who he belongs to!" With this speech she turned her back and marched off bristling.

Gerald and Harry watched her go off around the corner of the house. Gerald sighed. "She's right," he said. "She should decide for herself. We can't tell her. But we're all in an awful mess."

His mother's voice called him and he and Harry went into the house. Ma was standing with her pocketbook in her hand and Pa was beside her, her white coat over his arm.

"Oh there you are, dears! We are running off now — we're late. — Why, Gerald, is anything the matter?"

Gerald smiled a little uncertainly. "No — at least there is, but it's all very complicated and we'll tell you about it tomorrow."

"Well, if you're sure it can wait — " Ma glanced at the clock. "Sure it'll be all right till tomorrow?"

"Sure," said Gerald.

"John has had his supper and Saada is putting him to bed now. You'll see that Danny settles down after supper?"

"Yes," said Gerald. "He'll be all right."

His mother kissed the boys good night, and followed Pa down the long stairs. At the foot she hesitated and waved again. Gerald watched them go with a queer feeling in the pit of his stomach.

"I wish they didn't have to go out tonight," he said to Harry.

"Me too," replied Harry.

"We'll have to talk to Danny," sighed Gerald.

"Couldn't we wait till tomorrow and let Ma and Pa talk to him?" asked Harry.

"No," said Gerald. "It's not good to let this go on hanging. He'll probably be relieved to tell us about it anyway."

Fitny had set up a card table for the three boys on the back porch. Ordinarily it was fun to eat out there, with the cliffs behind them turning rosy-red in the setting sun. But tonight it seemed a little lonely. A frog was croaking in the pool below the house, and Gerald thought to himself, It's getting dark early these days. Summer is almost over. Harry's thoughts were hardly more cheerful. He was thinking, Pa and Ma won't be home till very late, and the Bixtons are going to be furious, and Boadie is mad at us.

Danny's thoughts were not so dismal. He was wondering if it would be all right to rename a dog "Danny," after himself. This happy train of thought was interrupted by Gerald's voice.

"Danny, we know about Bouncy. We asked Boadie and she had to tell us."

Danny smiled. "Isn't it nice? Now we have a dog."

Gerald tore off a piece of bread and buttered it slowly. "Danny, he isn't our dog. He belongs to the Bixtons."

"But he ran away," explained Danny.

"You and Boadie made him run away," corrected Gerald. His curiosity got the better of him. "How did you do it?" he asked.

"He ran away by himself," repeated Danny stoutly. "We just showed him how. There was a little hole in the wall. We played with him and talked to him through the hole. And we gave him some meatball. And finally he came out through the hole and played with us a long time. When we had to go home he followed us all by himself! We told him to go back through the hole but he kept following us."

"Where is he now?" asked Gerald.

Danny was silent.

"Where is he?" repeated Gerald.

"I promised Boadie not to tell," said Danny soberly.

Gerald took a new tack. "Danny," he said, "if you found Mrs. Bixton's pocketbook lying on the road and you knew it was hers, would you keep it?"

Danny looked shocked. "No! I'd take it back to her."

"I know," said Gerald. "Well, you found Edmund's puppy outside his yard, but it's still Edmund's puppy."

Danny looked unhappy. "Do we have to take him back?"

"I don't know what else we can do," said Gerald.

"Maybe they'll let us keep him!" said Danny hopefully.

"I wouldn't count on it," replied his brother. "You'd better go to bed now, Danny. Fitny wants to clear the table. Forget about all this tonight and go to sleep. Tomorrow we'll figure it out." He gave Danny a brotherly pat on the shoulder, and Harry did the same.

"We'll come and see you when you've brushed your teeth. Get into your pajamas."

Gerald helped Fitny fold up the bridge table and carried it in for her. While she closed the heavy back door and bolted it, he and Harry set the parcheesi board out on the table in the court. Fitny had lit the kerosene lamp and the green shade cast a friendly light over the board, even though the last rays of rose color still shone in the sky through the big windows overlooking the sea.

Suddenly the big knocker on the front door pounded loudly. Gerald and Harry looked at each other and jumped up. "I'll take the lamp," said Gerald. "You unlock the door."

The big door swung wide and the lamp shone on the faces of Mrs. Bixton and Edmund. Gerald and Harry looked at each other in consternation. Edmund was very angry.

"We've come to get my dog!" he said loudly.

"There *must* be a misunderstanding," said Mrs. Bixton. "Are your parents here?"

"There's no misunderstanding!" said Edmund. "A fine act they put on this afternoon, hunting for the dog! A woman from the village just told our cook that she saw your brother Danny carrying him down the road. Where is he?"

"I'm here," said Danny, wedging himself in between Gerald and Harry. He was in his pajamas. "I did carry your dog down the road. But he ran away by himself. He wanted to follow me. And I think when a dog wants to follow somebody home, that person ought to keep him. Don't you?" he asked, turning to Mrs. Bixton.

She smiled at him and seemed about to answer, but Edmund broke in.

"You get him and give him to me right now!"

Danny looked at him and said solemnly, "When you're sad you cry and yell, don't you? And your mother gives you what you want."

Edmund glared at him.

Danny asked him, "Is this lady your mother?"

"Yes dear," replied Mrs. Bixton.

Danny's lips began to quiver. "I'm littler than Edmund, and if you take my dog away, I'll cry."

"Shut up!" said Edmund. "Get that dog."

At this point an astonishing thing happened. Danny opened his mouth wide and roared. He cried and he screamed and the tears rolled down his cheeks. Gerald in alarm set the lamp down on the floor and putting his hands on Danny's shoulders tried to quiet him. But Danny was shaking with sobs from head to foot, and when Gerald touched him he only bellowed louder.

"Danny!" yelled Gerald. "Do be quiet! Hush up!"

Danny only sobbed harder and increased the volume of his screams. Edmund backed out of the door in alarm, and Fitny came flying out from the kitchen, adding her screams to Danny's. She seemed to have the impression that Gerald was causing Danny's screams, for she grabbed his arm and began shaking him, shouting at him in Arabic. Mrs. Bixton trembling drew Harry out on to the front steps and shouted in his ear, "Please, please tell the dear little boy that he can have the dog. We had no idea he felt this way about it — did we, Edmund? We *want* him to keep it, don't we, Edmund dear?" Edmund nodded, and his mother took his arm and they fled down the stairs together. Harry entered and shut the front door behind him. He went up to Danny and screamed in his ear,

"SHUT UP! THEY SAY YOU CAN KEEP THE DOG!"

Like a faucet that has suddenly been turned off, Danny's noise ceased. Using the corner of his pajamas he wiped the tears off his cheeks. A big smile spread over his face, though his body still shook with sobs.

Gerald looked at him with disapproval. "Well, you got what you wanted, but I never saw you act like *that* before. What a big baby!"

Danny's smile did not fade. "Wasn't it awful?" he agreed shakily. "But it was the only way." He started off toward his bedroom, and paused at the door. "Do you think Ma will spank me?"

"Go to bed," said Gerald wearily.

Danny's thoughts were not repentant as he climbed into bed. They were simply occupied with something more interesting. It would be confusing, he thought, to have two Dannys around the house. Argos would be a fine name for a faithful dog.

THE FAMILY, dressed in bathrobes, was holding a council in the little parlor before breakfast. This was not an unusual gathering place, for in this oddly Americanized Arab house the large marble shower room was located nearly opposite the front door, and next to the little parlor. While some of the family took showers the rest of the family would wait their turns, towels over their arms, in the parlor, chatting or reading some of the bound volumes of *Harper's Magazine* or *St. Nicholas*.

Today no one was in the shower. Everyone was meeting to discuss the situation of the Bixtons' puppy. Pa said that in his opinion there were no two ways about it.

"Danny put on an act last night, and the Bixtons gave him the dog because of a misunderstanding."

He looked at Danny steadily and calmly. Danny looked back at him, just as calmly. His bare feet dangled from under his bathrobe, and he looked very small and solid sitting on the straight chair by the window.

"You have to get things straight, Danny. March right up and apologize to the lady for the scene you made last night. Then leave it up to her."

"But I really *felt* that way about losing the puppy, Pa. I just let go."

"And how!" murmured Gerald, who was glad that things were off his shoulders this morning.

"Sure you did," replied Pa. "But we'll have none of that sort of behavior around here." He paused, and then went on, "She gave you that dog because she had to. You might as well have pointed a revolver at the dear lady."

"But Pa, I promised Boadie not to tell where he is. What about her?"

"You'll have to see Boadie first then and straighten it out. Tell her the Bixtons already know you have the dog. She wasn't in on this scene last night, was she?"

"Oh no. That was all my own idea," said Danny.

"Well, I wouldn't be proud of it," said his father. "Now go along and get your baths, everybody."

He moved over to the organ and began playing "Shall We Gather at the River?"

An hour later the three boys were on their way down to Boadie's house when they saw her red head appearing above the terrace near the outdoor cistern.

She saw them as they saw her and began, "You needn't think I've repented of my sins because I haven't, but I just can't stay mad."

"A lot has happened since we saw you," replied Gerald. "The Bixtons know that you and Danny have the puppy; somebody saw Danny carrying him, and told them."

"Not the nice man!" exclaimed Danny. "He promised he wouldn't tell!"

"It was a woman who told," said Gerald.

Boadie was staring at Danny.

"What man?" she demanded. "I thought nobody knew about Bouncy except you and me."

Danny sighed. "I forgot to tell you. After lunch yesterday when people were having their naps or reading, I went up to you-know-where to see if Bouncy was all right."

"The cave," said Boadie shortly. "Might as well tell them now."

"So that's why you were so anxious to take Miss Dunbar to Slanty Rocks!" exclaimed Gerald. "Instead of going back to the cave."

Boadie nodded. "Go on, Danny."

"So when I got to the cave I untied Bouncy and let him run around outside and play a little. He likes to play now. When I looked up I saw a man watching us. At first I was scared, sort of, but he was smiling and had a nice face. So we got to talking. He sat on the stone by the door of the little house."

"Was he an Arab?" asked Boadie.

"Yes," said Danny. "First we talked in English and then we talked in Arabic. He likes dogs. I told him all about Bouncy and he promised not to tell."

"What was his name?" asked Harry.

"I don't know," replied Danny. "I asked him but he didn't hear me. He was taking a pricker out of Bouncy's paw, and I was too shy to ask him again."

"Well you shouldn't go up there alone," said Gerald. "And you should never talk to strangers."

"I wasn't alone," replied Danny gravely. "I had a dog with me. And he's not a stranger; he's nice. He's my friend."

Gerald and Harry exchanged a puzzled glance. They were all walking back slowly toward the house.

"So the Bixtons have taken that poor little dog back again?" asked Boadie.

"No," said Harry quickly. "They came last night to get him. Pa and Ma were out, and Edmund was very mad, and — "

"And so I yelled and screamed and Mrs. Bixton said I could keep the dog!" burst in Danny excitedly.

"Good boy!" exclaimed Boadie joyously. "Where is he?"

"*But,*" said Gerald taking up the narrative, "Pa says Danny's got to go and apologize to Mrs. Bixton this morning and offer to give the dog back. We mustn't keep him under false pretenses."

Boadie shook her head.

"What a family! — I'll go with you," she said suddenly. "If Mrs. Bixton's a gentleman she'll insist on your keeping him. If she isn't, I'm going to get that dog myself by hook or by crook. Sometimes," she added looking reflectively at the boys, "I can see why George the Third let the American colonies go."

Mrs. Bixton was a gentleman. Even Edmund showed faint symptoms of becoming one when the children arrived and explained their errand. His mother insisted that Danny keep the puppy, but it was Edmund's own idea to give Danny the little dish and the basket which belonged to Bouncy. Danny followed him out to the kitchen steps to get them. As Edmund handed them to him Danny blushed a little.

"I'm sorry I yelled so much last night. I don't usually." He had made his formal apology to Mrs. Bixton earlier, but this was strictly between Edmund and himself.

Edmund said solemnly to the small boy in front of him, "Probably it's good you did. You sounded awful. I yell too sometimes. I don't think I will any more."

"You're pretty big to yell," said Danny gravely.

"I know it. And you act pretty big for your size."

"Thanks," said Danny. "Not last night though."

"What a noise!" agreed Edmund.

As they rejoined the others in the living room, Danny showed the things to Gerald, in whose arms Danny had left the puppy.

"Eddie says we can keep these."

Gerald gave Edmund an odd glance.

"Would you like to come along with us?" he asked.

Edmund hesitated. "Yeah," he said. "Thanks."

Danny walked in front, carrying the puppy "so his feet won't get dusty." Edmund was on his left, and Gerald was on his right. Boadie walked a yard or two behind, muttering to Harry.

"I don't see why Gerald had to ask him to come along. Just because he gave Danny the dog that he didn't want anyway."

Harry let her go on muttering. It might be interesting, he thought, to see what Edmund was really like. As for Boadie, she had just that morning admitted that she couldn't stay mad.

"What does Gerald expect to do — show him the secret cave and *everything?*" asked Boadie.

"Sh!" warned Harry. "No. He wouldn't do that without our permission. We could just as well let him see what we're doing to the ruined house, though. That's no secret anyway." He paused as a disquieting thought came back to him. "I don't like the idea of that strange man hanging around though — even if he does like dogs."

"Me either," said Boadie ungrammatically.

In a few minutes the group had arrived at the boys' house. While everybody else sat in an admiring circle around the puppy, under the shade of the pines, Danny ran into the house to tell the good news to his parents. Ma came out from the storeroom, with a list in one hand, and Pa needed no persuasion to leave some medical notes which he was sorting on the dining table. With Danny they went out to join the puppy's audience and to thank Edmund. They found John already there, so interested in the new dog that he forgot to be embarrassed in the presence of Edmund and Boadie.

"By the way, Boadie," asked Harry, "how come Miss Dunbar let you off from your lessons today?"

"She just didn't say anything," replied Boadie. "I told her that moral issues were involved and I wouldn't be able to concentrate. Dunbar's a good egg."

"She's too easy on you," remarked Gerald.

Boadie smiled. "You don't know Dunbar. What I miss this morning I'll make up this afternoon."

"Same with us," remarked Gerald glumly.

His parents, deaf to these pathetic remarks, were watching the puppy awkwardly trying to catch a scurrying ant with one paw.

"What did you say his name was?" asked Pa.

Danny spoke quickly. "His name was Bouncy. But he's growing up now and I'm giving him another name. Now his name is Argos."

"Argos," repeated Pa. "Why, Danny?"

"He was the faithful dog who knew who Useless was when he came home."

"He's talking about Ulysses," said Gerald. "Miss Dunbar told us about him. But I don't remember about the dog."

"He's right," said Pa. "And it's a good name."

"By the way, Ma," said Gerald, "didn't you say that there were some more odds and ends of furniture that we could have for the little house?"

Ma nodded. Gerald turned to Boadie and Harry. "Let's tell Edmund. While he's here we've got an extra person to carry stuff up."

Even Boadie nodded at this practical suggestion.

"There's this little house on the mountain," explained Gerald to Edmund. He looked up and pointed it out. "See it up there? It's in ruins, but we've cleaned

it out and we're going to fix it up as a place to play in. Want to help?"

Edmund gazed up at the house a few moments without replying. He seemed to hesitate a bit, and looked over at Boadie, who suddenly seemed deeply absorbed in studying the ants.

"Well, I guess so," said Edmund. "You're sure that house is O.K.? I heard a funny noise there once."

There was an embarrassed silence.

"Probably you heard some goat or donkey," said Ma helpfully. She had been rescuing the puppy from John's too loving embrace, and had not followed the conversation very closely. "Now what in the world is funny about that?" she asked, looking wonderingly at Harry who was choking with delight.

"Sometimes they *sound* near by when they're really far away," she continued kindly, to Edmund. "It's the mountain air."

Edmund still looked a little puzzled, but he seemed satisfied, and the others were content not to explain any further either to Ma or to Edmund.

Danny was left in charge of Argos while Pa went back to his notes and the others followed Ma up the narrow stairs into the huge old attic. Before long a heavily laden procession was starting up the hill. Boadie led the way, carrying an old kitchen chair. Harry followed, with a rocking chair that had lost one rocker. Danny, the third in the procession, was given the duty of escorting, persuading, boosting and pushing little Argos up the hill. This was a slow job as Argos

found many side interests to explore, and Danny soon stepped aside to let Gerald and Edmund pass. Between them they were carrying an old wooden table up the hill. Ma had demurred when the boys said they wanted it.

"But it's such a load to carry, and what on earth will you do with it once you have it up there?"

"It'll be the most useful thing we've got," said Gerald. "We can use it to sit on, or to sit under in case of rain (the rains will begin soon, you know) or for an operating table, or we can set it on its side to make a partition in the house. We can even use it just as a table, to put food on. Then Danny's board-table can be a bench."

Eventually the whole cavalcade arrived at the ruined house. A long argument ensued. Each person, it appeared, had a different opinion as to how the furniture should be arranged. Gerald said the proper place for a table was in the middle of the room. Harry said he thought it looked more artistic against the back wall — "with a dish of fruit on it or something." Boadie suggested a compromise.

"Why not try it different ways till we see where we like it? We'll try Harry's way first because we won't always be bumping into it."

So the table was set against the back wall, Danny's low board bench was moved just under the large, odd window, Harry's rocker was placed by the door and the kitchen chair by another window. Boadie completed the picture by appearing with Danny's vinegar bottle into which she had stuck a few sprays of heather. This she set on the table. Then she stepped back and admired the little room.

"All we need here now," slowly said Edmund, who had not joined in the discussion before, "is a roof."

"Well we can't make a roof, so that's that," said Boadie.

"Not a real roof," said Edmund. "But haven't you seen the little roofs they make around here, for porches and things, out of branches and dried leaves? We could make one like that, just for the shade."

"We'll look around up among the pine trees," said Gerald, "for dead branches. The bigger the better. Drag them down here. We can't cut any, but there'll be plenty of dead ones if we look. I saw a big one hanging in the big pine on the cliff the other day."

"I'll get that one," offered Edmund.

"O.K. I'll come show it to you," said Gerald.

Leaving the others to search around above the house, they started off together. There was a question that had been bothering Gerald, and he brought it out abruptly as they walked along.

"Eddie, why did you act so mean to your dog?"

"I don't know," replied Edmund miserably. "I was sore at everybody, I guess. I couldn't kick everybody so I kicked him."

"Why were you sore?"

Edmund kept walking along and did not look at Gerald, but he spoke earnestly. "Listen. Nobody ever liked me so why should I like anybody? Mother was the only one, but she likes my stepfather now."

"Can't she like both of you?" demanded Gerald impatiently. "Gosh, my mother likes my father but she's got a lot of us kids to like too. A fine thing it would be if each one of us wanted her not to like the others!"

"Well," said Edmund, "it's not just my mother. Other kids don't like me either. You didn't yourself."

"I'll say I didn't!" agreed Gerald heartily. "All those dopey jokes — putting thistles on chairs and so on — that's no way to make friends. And gee, Eddie, you look terrible. Why don't you cut your hair? And act like a fellow instead of a baby?"

Edmund turned around angrily, but Gerald only grinned at him.

"And learn to laugh at yourself."

Edmund smiled reluctantly. They were getting near the pine tree.

"There's the brown branch — up near the top. See it?" asked Gerald. "Here's my knife. You may need it. I'm going back now to help the others."

Edmund went on to the base of the pine. Putting his arms around the trunk he started to shinny up. Then he changed his mind, and walking away a few steps he attempted the running jump approach. The first time he was unsuccessful, but at last he got his leg over the branch and heaved himself up to a sitting position.

"Well done!" said a muffled voice in the branches over his head.

He looked up in surprise and saw Miss Dunbar looking down at him approvingly, a pencil in her mouth. She was peering over the top of her glasses, which looked as though they might drop off at any moment. On her lap was a tablet of some sort, and stuck in her hair over her ear was another pencil; she appeared to be sketching.

Removing the pencil from her mouth and waving it to emphasize her remarks, she added, "Next time take a bit longer run first — then more of a snap when you leap up. You're doing very well."

"Thanks," said Edmund.

"You're quite welcome," replied Miss Dunbar kindly.

"What are you doing up there?" asked Edmund.

"Sketching," was the reply. "Quite a nice effect you get from up here — just blue sea and sky seen through the pine needles and all. Did you bring sketching things?"

"No," Edmund replied, a little surprised. Miss Dunbar spoke as if sketching things were a natural part of tree climbers' equipment.

"Bring some next time," suggested Miss Dunbar. "Have a go at it."

"I can't draw," said Edmund.

"Neither can I," was the response. "But I *do*. And it's good fun. In a tree anyway. Nobody can hang about watching you over your shoulder."

Edmund could think of nothing to say. He had just been hoping she would show him her sketch, but he decided now not to ask her. He looked around to find the dead branch he had come for.

"I say," the amiable voice went on, "would you like a go at this now for a bit? I have two sketching pads with me, and you may have one, and borrow the pencils. I shall rest and read a little while."

"I couldn't — " began Edmund.

"Nonsense," replied Miss Dunbar cheerfully. "You've never tried, have you?"

She leaned over, handing down the pad.

"No, but — "

"Try anyway! I won't look at what you do. Simple. Pine needles green lines. Sky light blue. Sea deeper blue. Mountains purple. Light places very light — shadows dark, very dark. There you are! Some days you'll want to do everything differently. Pine needles purple. Mountains black. Sea pink. People look at it and say, 'Very interesting. Full of feeling, that.' Fun, what?"

She chuckled and Edmund found himself grinning as he reached for the pencils.

It was a bit difficult at first balancing himself in the tree with the pad on his knees, but before long he wedged himself into a secure position. He glanced up at Miss Dunbar, but she had opened her book and seemed to have forgotten all about him. He would "have a go" at it for a few minutes anyway.

Meanwhile Gerald had gone back to the little pine trees on the other end of the ridge, where he met Harry and Boadie. Already they had collected a pile of dead branches.

Gerald looked around and asked Harry, "Where's Danny?"

"Back at the ruined house," said Harry. "Why?"

"You shouldn't leave him all alone like that," said Gerald crossly. "I thought one of you would have the sense to stay near by."

"He's all right," said Harry. But he began to feel uneasy and his reply too was a little cross. "You left him too," he said. "You said to get branches and there are hardly any trees near here."

"Come on!" said Boadie starting ahead. "I'll rush on ahead to see that he's all right and you can take your time bringing the branches."

But Gerald and Harry were both worried by this time, and picking up a branch apiece they hurried along not far behind Boadie. They could see her on ahead when she reached the ledge above the little ruined house. Their anxiety was increased when she suddenly stopped short there, looking down. Then she called sharply, "Danny!" and disappeared, dropping down over the ledge. In a moment or two they also had reached the ledge and stopped short.

Below them were Boadie and Danny, facing them; but a man was with them, his back turned toward the boys as they stood there.

"It must be Danny's friend!" whispered Harry.

Boadie saw them and waved.

"There they are!" she explained to Danny and the other person.

The tall man turned around and they recognized the kindly, tired face of Mr. Haddad, the gentleman who was staying with Sheikh Mohammed. Gerald and Harry waved back, and a short scramble brought them down to the terrace where the others stood.

"These are my brothers," said Danny with a grand gesture.

"How do you do, Mr. Haddad?" said Gerald.

Danny looked disappointed. "I didn't know you knew each other. This is my friend. He likes dogs."

Mr. Haddad smiled. "I did not know that you were brothers. I visited your father a few days ago."

"How do you like this house, Mr. Haddad?" asked Harry.

Mr. Haddad looked in at the little house. He seemed to notice everything, even the little sprays of heather on the table. He smiled, and when he answered his voice was very soft.

"I like your little house," he said quietly. "It has a welcoming look. May I sit down?"

"Of course!" said Boadie. "You're our first caller — since we got our furniture, I mean."

Mr. Haddad insisted that Boadie must sit down first, so she chose the rocking chair. It sagged a little on the side where the rocker was missing, but it looked very elegant. Mr. Haddad sat down on the kitchen chair. Danny sat cross-legged on the floor next to Argos, while Gerald and Harry lowered themselves cautiously on to Danny's board bench. "You will have to excuse us," said Boadie in her most ladylike tone; "we are sorry that we have no coffee to offer you. You see we just moved in."

"Please don't trouble yourself about that," replied Mr. Haddad with equal elegance; "I quite understand."

Then they both grinned at each other. Danny happily turned a somersault on the matting, to the indignation of Argos who had to sniff him all over from head to toe right afterwards, to make sure it was the same boy.

Mr. Haddad laughed as he watched them. Then he suddenly grew sober.

"This is a nice place to play," he said. "But it seems rather lonely for a place to live. Do you know anything about the people who lived here before?"

"It was an old lady," answered Gerald. "We heard about her from Miss Mariam. She lived here for years all alone."

"How did that happen?" asked Mr. Haddad.

He seemed so interested that Gerald replied, "I'll tell you the whole story, just as Miss Mariam told us."

"And we'll help," said Harry eagerly. "If you forget anything."

"I'm not going to forget anything," replied Gerald with dignity.

But it seemed that he did; anyway Harry and Boadie kept interrupting the story with details and comments.

"I was coming to that," protested Gerald once or twice. "You're rushing the story."

But finally the whole story was told. The children looked eagerly at Mr. Haddad to see what he thought about it. But it seemed that he had lost interest, or perhaps he had not been paying attention at all to the story. He was looking down at the valley below, where a far-off stretch of white road ended in a little U-shaped curve and lost itself around the mountain. Everyone was silent for a minute. The sweet smell of sage and thyme blew in and through the old house.

Again Boadie felt a sort of sadness connected with the place. She sighed and remarked, "It must have been so lonely for her; here all those years by herself."

Mr. Haddad turned his head slowly and looked across at Boadie. His face looked tired still, but she noticed how clear his deep brown eyes were. He shook his head.

"No, she was not alone here. She never did live by herself. Someone else was here with her all that time."

Everyone was very still. The dry thistles rustled in the breeze.

Then Harry whispered, "Not — you?"

"Yes," replied the man quietly. "I was here with my mother all the time."

Your name is Butrus?" asked Gerald, still hardly able to believe what he was hearing.

The visitor nodded. "Butrus Haddad it is now. But Haddad is not my real name. Do you know what Haddad means in Arabic?"

"Smith," said Gerald.

Butrus smiled. "That's right. And there are almost as many Haddads around here as there are Smiths in Western countries. So it seemed like a good name to take when I decided to disappear."

"But why did you disappear?" demanded Harry.

The tall man looked thoughtfully at him. "How much do you children know about our country here, and the people who govern us?"

"Not too much," admitted Gerald. "I know that nobody liked it much when the Turks were ruling the country. I guess no country likes to be ruled by another. Then the Turks left at the end of the war."

" — And the British troops marched in!" burst in Harry excitedly. "We saw them marching into Beirut! That was last year."

"So the Arabs have an independent nation here," contributed Boadie.

Butrus shook his head.

"Not yet," he said sadly. "The French are taking control of the country, but they say we shall have our independence someday. It has been a long struggle."

He paused, and the children waited.

"Even twenty-five years ago," he went on in a moment, "many of us young men were working for our independence. I was young then, and very outspoken about my ideas. Finally I aroused the notice of the police. Then our leaders told me I could help my country more if Butrus Sidani disappeared. I had a little piece of land on the mountain, with a cave which no one else knew about." He smiled at Danny. "Where your little dog was staying. Someday you must tell me how you found my cave!

"So I built the house next to the cave. I had to tell my mother the whole plan first, for she was a necessary part of it. I was to disappear, but I was to go on living here in the cave. At night I could go about the country, carrying messages and gathering information. But I continued to live secretly here, with my mother."

"That extra dish and extra bedding that she had always ready — " Boadie broke in.

Mr. Haddad nodded. "They were used every day. I used them."

"And that big window toward the cliff — "

"Sometimes late in the day or early in the morning I could sit outside the cave entrance in the air. From that spot I could see the pathway if the front door was left open. Sometimes in the evening I would sit in the house here with my mother. It was easy to leap over that low window sill and into the cave if we heard anyone." He smiled. "Several times a jackal running past the house would send me leaping through that window and into the cave!"

He rose from his chair and stood in the doorway looking down at the sea.

"I don't think my mother ever regretted her decision. She chose a life of danger for her country. She could not read or write, but she was a patriotic woman and very brave." He turned and looked at the children. "She missed her friends in the village, I know. She knew they thought she was crazy, but it was better so because they left us alone here. Most of all I think she missed the children. She knew it was better for them not to come here, because sooner or later children discover everything." He smiled at the four adventurers. "Don't they?"

The children smiled.

"And now," concluded Butrus, "I can't help feeling that she would be glad to know that the children are here again. All this — " he waved his hand at the furnishings in the little house — "she would like this, and I do too."

"Were you here when she died?" asked Gerald in a low tone.

"I was with her. She was not ill very long, and to the end she did not regret what she had done. When she died I had to leave. It was hard, going like that, but she had made me promise to waste no time if it ever happened. That night I hurriedly took all my personal belongings and left the cave forever."

"Not *all*," corrected Gerald.

Butrus looked surprised. "What do you mean?"

"You left a coat and some old shoes in an oil jar buried in the cave," Gerald reminded him.

Butrus laughed. "You didn't miss anything, did you? I hadn't thought about that old jar for years. I suppose I stuffed those things in there so they wouldn't be found. I couldn't carry everything with me."

"How long ago was all that?" asked Boadie.

"Twenty years," said Butrus with a sigh. "A long time to be away from home."

Danny looked up suddenly. "Just like Useless."

Gerald scowled at him a little. "Ulysses."

Mr. Haddad glanced at him and held out his hand to Argos. The puppy trotted over to him, wagging his tail. The man scratched the little head gently while the tail wagged even harder.

"Do the village people know you are back?" asked Gerald suddenly.

Butrus shook his head. "I don't know what they would think about me. Maybe they have all forgotten us anyway."

"Not Miss Mariam!" said Harry earnestly. "And she says lots of the people remember you. They like you. She says you were an obstinate young man and liked to argue."

"Shut up," reproved Gerald.

"Never mind," said Mr. Haddad good-naturedly. "She's right, too. Who is this Miss Mariam?"

"Mishalany is her name," said Gerald.

Mr. Haddad's face brightened. "I remember them. She was a little girl in those days. Your age," he said looking at Danny. "I don't remember her much. But I remember her mother well. She was my mother's best friend, before — before things changed. Mrs. Mishalany was the last one of the village women to call on my mother."

"Does the Sheikh know who you are?" asked Gerald.

Butrus smiled. "I shouldn't wonder. I haven't told him, but the Sheikh generally guesses things. — By the way," he said, looking at his watch, "don't you children ever eat? It's twelve o'clock and I must be going down the hill. May I come back again?"

"Of course!"

"Please come soon!" said the children in unison.

The enthusiastic chorus pleased the visitor, and he waved cheerfully to them as he started down the path.

Gerald turned to the others with a puzzled look.

"What in the world has happened to Edmund?" he asked.

"Where did you leave him?" asked Harry.

"He was just going into the pine tree to get a branch and come right back," said Gerald with a look of growing dismay. "Gee, you don't suppose he's broken his leg or something?"

He and Harry started running up the path toward the pine.

"Edmund! Hey Eddie!" called Gerald, pausing and making his hands into a megaphone.

An answering call came from the distant pine.

"Here I am! Coming!" came the answer.

A moment later the boys saw Edmund dangling from the lowest branch; then he dropped to the ground. Presently a second figure, taller, and familiar, with long flowing trousers dangled and dropped, and the two came walking toward them.

"Miss Dunbar!" murmured Harry.

Edmund was dragging a huge pine branch behind him as he came. As he and Miss Dunbar drew nearer Gerald spoke to them.

"Good morning, Miss Dunbar. Look, Eddie, what happened to you? Couldn't you get the branch loose?"

"Oh, Miss Dunbar was there and we just got to talking," said Edmund vaguely.

"Edmund tells me that the little ruined house is going to have a roof," remarked Miss Dunbar.

"We're collecting the stuff," said Harry, "but we must stop now because it's noon."

They met Boadie and Danny where the path went nearest to the little house. Boadie turned to Edmund and inquired politely, "Your leg's all right?"

"Sure," replied Edmund, a little mystified.

"We thought you might have broken one. I say, what's that you have under your arm?"

Edmund shifted a piece of paper to his other hand.

"Nothing much," he said.

"Well, I just wondered —"

"Dorothy!" Miss Dunbar spoke a little sharply, and Boadie was silent.

"Oh gee, I don't mind," said Edmund sheepishly. "It's just that the picture isn't any good. Miss Dunbar lent me a pad and I sketched the view. You can look at it. Just for a laugh. It's awful."

He held out the picture and Boadie examined it critically.

"It's not bad," said she. "You should see my sketching. It's ten times more ghastly than yours," she said flatteringly.

"Couldn't be," remarked Edmund. "This doesn't look like anything."

"Well you're no genius," conceded Boadie. "What did you expect on your first try — a bally masterpiece?" She examined it again. "Now that green line there — there's a pine needle that really looks like a pine needle. Jolly good, that." Edmund's ears grew red with pleasure.

The group had been moving down the mountainside as they talked.

"I have to turn off here," said Edmund, stopping halfway down the mountain. "It's shorter for me to cut over across from here."

"See you this afternoon?" asked Gerald.

"Yes, I'll bring some tools along. How soon?"

"Right after lunch!" said Boadie. "It'll take quite a while to put the roof on."

"Ahem!" remarked Miss Dunbar.

"Oh, of course! I forgot!" groaned Boadie. "Around tea time then. I have to do my lessons first."

"So do we," Gerald assured her.

"Later then," said Edmund. "Goodbye till this after!"

"Bye, Eddie!"

"Bye, Ed!"

"Toodle-oo, Edmundo my boy!"

As the remainder of the party continued down the path, Boadie inquired, "Are we going to tell Edmund about the secret cave?"

"Not just yet," said Gerald, "We'll wait a while and see how he is. He's going to have to learn to laugh at himself, you know, first. All those ghosts and volcanoes and things he thought he heard." Gerald smiled a little and then was serious again. "I have an idea though, that Eddie's going to be O.K."

They had come to where the path divided. Miss Dunbar started ahead off the path to the right, and Gerald and Harry and Danny paused to wave to Boadie as she turned off. Suddenly Harry called her back.

"Boadie, you know something? You're as good as a boy in lots of ways."

Boadie started to bristle, then she realized that this speech was intended as a compliment.

"Well thanks," she said. "And you boys have almost as much sense as if you'd been girls."

But Harry had not finished. "I have something here that I don't show many people. In fact Danny's only seen it a couple of times. I consider it an honor." He took a small tin box marked "Bayer's Aspirin" out of his pocket.

"More hair?" inquired Boadie.

"Not this," said Harry.

"Can I look too?" asked Danny.

"You may," said Harry. He opened the little box.

"Goodness! What are they?" asked Boadie peering in.

"My teeth," said Harry. "I've saved every one that came out. Aren't they interesting?"

"Can I hold them?" asked Danny respectfully.

"No, you might drop them," was the reply. "I'll hold them while you look. If you lose these they can't be replaced."

For a moment the four heads were bent over the box in silence. Then Harry closed the box.

"'Aspirin,'" read Boadie aloud. "Another aspirin box. I expect your mother must use a lot of aspirin with four boys around."

Really Boadie could be very trying.

Lunch in the boys' household was a very interesting meal today. The mystery of the cave had to be explained to their parents, who were very interested to learn that Mr. Haddad had turned out to be the long-vanished Butrus.

"How nice it was that you had cleared up the little house and even furnished it a bit," said Ma, "so that the place didn't seem quite so desolate when he returned. You say he didn't mind your having used the house?"

"He liked it," said Harry.

"There seems no reason for his keeping his secret any longer," remarked the boys' mother to their father. "Do you suppose he'll be letting his old friends in the village know that he's back?"

"I'm sure he will," replied Pa. "And the Sheikh will probably give a big party in his honor, for all the village. Butrus is going to learn fast that the Shemlan people don't forget their friends."

"Do you know," said Ma softly, "I think we'll have a little celebration of our own tonight, on the mountain. We'll invite just the Sheikh and Mr. Haddad, and we'll have supper on top of the mountain where we can watch the moon rise. What do you think of that?"

"YEA! ! !" shouted Gerald and Harry together.

"And Danny, and me?" asked John.

His mother smiled at him.

"Ask Pa. You always fall asleep at supper picnics, and he has to carry you down the mountain."

John looked earnestly at his father.

"I'll carry some baskets up the mountain if you'll carry me down, Pa," he offered. "If I fall asleep. Maybe I won't tonight. I'm not sleepy at all."

Pa looked at him thoughtfully.

"You weigh a lot for three years old. How many sandwiches are you planning to eat?"

"Not many," said John quickly. "Only about six. Or seven — And a few other things," he added honestly.

"I guess we can manage," said Pa.

"How about Boadie and Miss Dunbar?" asked Gerald.

"Of course they must come," agreed his mother.

"And Edmund?" asked Danny.

Gerald and Harry were silent. Their mother glanced at their father.

"Well, what do you boys think?" she asked.

Harry made a face and then admitted, "We'd probably better ask him. I think he's really doing the best he can."

Their father stood up to carve the watermelon. He revolved it slowly on the platter till he found the best place to make the incision. The boys' eyes were on the melon as it split neatly into two halves.

"He really is trying," said Gerald. "He's going to come and work on the roof this afternoon."

Usually the boys found it very hard to wait when a picnic supper was planned. But today the afternoon had passed quickly. Boadie and Edmund had arrived almost at the same time. The tea things were already set out on the porch, but the whole roofing party had decided to take a cooky apiece and start up the mountain. They could work until nearly sunset, when the grownups would arrive. They had climbed the mountain, carrying between them several old beams which Pa had found for them stacked in the woodshed. Danny carried a coil of wire and again had charge of coaxing Argos up the hill.

"Why not leave him behind this time?" suggested Gerald. "It's such a job getting him up the mountain."

Danny shook his head. "I'll get him up. He wants to come with us."

So Argos and Danny had followed the others at a distance. And now Gerald and Edmund were perched on top of the front wall and the side wall of the little house, while Harry and Boadie handed up the beams and the branches which they had collected on the mountain, and gave directions from below. In the midst of the operations Boadie paused and beckoned to Harry. He followed her around the house. Boadie waited for him just out of sight of the others, a broad smile on her face.

"What do you think of Edmund's haircut?" she asked.

"Is it cut?" asked Harry vaguely. "I hadn't noticed."

"It certainly is," she replied. "He looks like a different boy."

Harry started around the house for a look. Edmund's head was outlined against the blue sky. It was true; his hair had been practically shaved off to a line along the middle of his ears; above that it sprouted out again to a moderate length; but the canopy of hair which used to hang over his forehead was gone.

Harry disappeared again around the corner of the house to where Boadie was still waiting.

"Abdou did it," he said briefly. "The village barber. I'd recognize one of his haircuts anywhere."

"He must have popped off and had it done before tea," said Boadie. "Good boy, what? Once he makes up his mind."

A roar from Gerald interrupted their dialogue and roused Danny, who had been sitting on the matting holding Argos curled up in his sailor hat.

"*Harry! Boadie!* Get back to work here." And the two went back to the roof raising.

By the time the sun was getting low and sending its long golden rays horizontally through the doorway of the little house, the children's work was finished. They moved back in an admiring and weary little group to the edge of the terrace to look at what they had done.

Early in the proceedings they had decided to roof over only half the house.

"We don't want to make it too dark inside," remarked Boadie. "After all, this is a playhouse. All we want is a good solid piece of shade, and then we'll leave the other half open so we can watch the clouds sail by over us."

"The open half of the house can be like the uncovered

courts they always used to have in the old Arab houses," added Harry. "Very historical."

"Very practical too," said Gerald dryly. "Seeing we have only enough beams and branches to cover one side."

Boadie had looked at him with a pained expression. "*Please.* Don't lower our conversation to such ordinary details."

Now the workmen looked with satisfaction on the results of their labor.

"It looks altogether different, doesn't it?" said Boadie· "Sort of safe and inviting."

Gerald put a hand on Edmund's shoulder.

"Good idea, Ed. You thought of it."

Edmund smiled. "Aw, everybody had a hand in it."

A low, trilling whistle from below made them all turn around.

"They're starting up with the picnic things!" exclaimed Gerald. "Come on — we'd better tear on down there and help them with the stuff." He turned to Boadie. "Look — we know you can carry things as well as we can, but do you mind staying here with Danny? Otherwise he'll have to come too, and if he comes Argos has to come, and by the time we all get started they'll be up here!"

"All right," said Boadie absently. She was staring down at the group gathered behind the house. "Isn't there an extra person there?"

The boys followed her gaze.

"It's another lady," groaned Gerald. "Miss Dunbar's starting ahead up the path with John, talking to the Sheikh. I hope it isn't some caller who's going to hold us up again. Come on, let's get started."

The headlong descent began, and Boadie and Danny

watched the boys hurtling down the mountain.

"How often do your brothers break their legs?" asked Boadie.

"Not ever that I know of," replied Danny casually.

"Hmm!" commented Boadie in a tone of incredulity.

The extra guest was Miss Mariam. She had not come as a caller to detain the picnic; she was an invited guest. Ma explained it to Gerald as she took him aside to give him the basket of sandwiches.

"After you left I remembered what Mr. Haddad had told you about Mrs. Mishalany and his mother; so I sent word to Miss Mariam and invited her to come along."

Gerald nodded his head in approval. Soon the whole party was starting up the hill, single file.

An hour or so later the picnickers were spread about in various positions of comfort and satisfaction. Blankets had been laid on the ground for the elders to sit on, but the children scorned these, preferring each to choose his own little rock or ledge. A deep rose color still lingered in the western sky but the mountainside looked dark already, and a large planet shone out over the sea. Now they could see the white moonlight spreading over the plain below and creeping up the foothills, though the full moon itself was still hidden from them by the crest of the mountain. The sweet scent of the heather rose in the night air.

"What a beautiful place this is!" murmured Boadie to Harry. "And what beautiful food! I'm so full I feel as if I was going to pop."

"What a romantic girl you are," replied Harry.

Gerald leaned across Boadie to whisper to Harry, "Did you notice Eddie passing the samboosics to Miss Mariam? Boy! what a change!"

"Yes, indeed," murmured Boadie admiringly. "Wonderful boys you are. A good influence on us all."

"Right," said Gerald. "You've improved a lot under our influence. Glad you're grateful to us."

"Of course there's a lot to work on yet," added Harry kindly. "Another summer with us and you'll be quite a different girl."

"Another summer with you is too much to ask of any girl." Boadie stretched luxuriously. "Another summer!" she repeated softly. "I'll be back — I'll promise you that."

Pa had taken his mouth organ out of his pocket and began to play very softly, "By the Light of the Moon." The boys joined in and sang the words:

"If you want to go to Shemlan, just come along with me, By the light, by the light of the moon."

As they finished singing Pa repeated the last line very softly on his mouth organ. The moonlight was striking the high rocks around them now, and as the last note faded softly away, suddenly a beautiful stream of soft notes came flooding from a little pine tree.

"It's a bird!" whispered Ma. "How wonderful."

"A bulbul," whispered the Sheikh.

Everyone was utterly still as the beautiful cascade of melody flowed around them in the moonlight. Finally it stopped, the bird gave a chirp or two, and there was silence again.

"Braheem!" called Gerald.

All the grownups looked startled as a figure in the moonlight detached itself from a rock near by.

"I'm sorry to intrude," apologized Braheem. "It's only that last night in the moonlight Latifa sang for the first time, and I thought you would like to — " His voice faded away in embarrassment as he realized what a large group he was addressing.

But Gerald led him up and introduced him to everyone. When he reached Sheikh Mohammed in the circle, the Sheikh smiled kindly at Braheem and said to Gerald, "I know Braheem and his family well."

Braheem's face lit up as he recognized the Sheikh, and stepping before him he bowed and kissed the Sheikh's hand.

"How is your father, Braheem?" asked the Sheikh.

"He's well, sir," replied the boy. "But it's been too long since you came to see us."

"It has," replied the Sheikh smiling. "I hardly recognized you, you're so tall."

When Braheem caught sight of Miss Dunbar he smiled with pleasure.

"Sitt Miss Dumba," he murmured.

Soon he was sitting with the boys.

"Can you call Latifa and introduce her to everybody?" asked Gerald. He smiled at the puzzlement on the faces of the grownups.

Braheem gave a whistle and Latifa obligingly flew down and settled on his knee.

"Make her sing again," begged Boadie.

"What did she say?" asked Braheem.

"She wants the bird to sing," translated Gerald.

Braheem waved to Gerald's father.

"Your father's music makes her sing. Perhaps he will play again."

Pa started softly on his mouth organ again, playing "Redwing." The bird on Braheem's knee listened intently. Presently a soft trill began. The bird tipped her head back and her throat puffed as the music rose and soon the full sweet sound of it poured out.

"There's the moon," whispered Boadie.

The brilliant disk was over the rim of the mountain now and the faces of the listeners were brightly illumined. Finally the bird was silent. Latifa hopped around a little on Braheem's knee and settled down to rest.

"She has finished her song and says it's the turn of the others now," remarked the Sheikh. "Braheem, my boy, you'll have to change her name. It's only the male bulbuls who sing; Latifa is really Latif."

"He doesn't seem to care much," said Gerald, for Latifa, or Latif, had fluffed himself into a comfortable ball on his master's knee, and seemed to have gone to sleep.

Like John, thought Harry looking over at his little brother curled up in his father's arms, with Pa's big red sweater over him. Ma had her arm around Danny who was leaning comfortably against her, half asleep. His sweater bulged and the small sleepy head of Argos stuck out of it, the chin resting on Danny's knee, the little ears contentedly laid back.

Ma had begun to hum softly. The tune was familiar and soon Miss Mariam and Gerald and Harry were singing too, while Pa's mouth organ played a soft accompaniment. It was not till they had reached the second verse that Harry suddenly seemed to hear the words they were singing, as if for the first time.

> " . . . *for this is heaven's border-land.*
> *Oh Beulah land . . .*
> *As on thy highest mount I stand*
> *I look away across the sea*
> *Where mansions are prepared for me . . .*"

Harry looked away across the sea, spread out far below in
the moonlight. Over there was America — "where mansions

are prepared for me." Some day he and Gerald would go
there to college. Pa and Ma always spoke of America as

home. Well, he didn't see how it could be more beautiful than this Beulah land, right here on the mountaintops of Lebanon. The mansions, wherever they were, in America or in heaven itself, could wait. He was in no hurry to grow up.